WISHING
SEASON

WISHING SEASON

ANICA MROSE RISSI

Quill Tree Books
An Imprint of HarperCollins*Publishers*

Quill Tree Books is an imprint of HarperCollins Publishers.

Wishing Season

Library of Congress Control Number: 2022946440
ISBN 978-0-06-325890-7

Typography by Andrea Vandergrift
23 24 25 26 27 LBC 5 4 3 2 1

First Edition

For Deer Isle, with love

1

The Question

At ten minutes past the usual time, the school bus rolled to its usual stop, opened its doors, and coughed out a girl. Her sneakers landed in the gravel with a crunch.

The girl paused, looking right for any cars coming up the tall hill—all clear—and crossed in front of the bus's flashing red lights. She hurried up the slope on the other side of the road, but as soon as the grassy ground evened out, her steps slowed.

She did not turn to wave at any friends as the bus grumbled along to the next stop. She didn't run to the door of the big white house, or even smile as she approached it. She hunched her shoulders, hooked her thumbs through the straps of her backpack, and braced for what she would find inside.

Two red-breasted nuthatches chirped on a nearby branch. "That poor girl," one said. "That poor, unfortunate child."

The other bird hopped closer. "She'll be all right."

"Will she?" the first wondered.

They tilted their heads and watched.

2

Messages from the Dead

Lily stood in the entryway and let the screen door bang shut behind her. She held her breath and listened for a reaction but was greeted only by silence. She sputtered her lips, making a sound like an impatient horse, and dropped her bag to the floor with a thunk, just to fill the enormous quiet.

Four months ago, if Lily let a door slam like that, she'd be scolded or given an eye roll. Four months ago, if Mom was busy when the twins got home from school, she'd still call out hello and give snack instructions, and come hear about their day in a minute. Four months ago, Lily rarely got off the school bus alone.

A lot could change in four months.

Lily used her foot to nudge her backpack out of the way and went into the kitchen. "How was the last day of school?" she asked aloud, because someone should, and the only sign of her mom was the half-eaten breakfast abandoned on the counter. Lily dumped the soggy cereal and put the bowl and spoon in the sink.

"It was fine," she answered, keeping her tone light and easy. "Nothing exciting until the end, when some fuzzbutt pulled the fire alarm, so we were late getting onto the buses."

There was a new stack of mail on top of the old stack—evidence Mom had gone at least as far as the mailbox that day—and Lily riffled through it. Junk, bill, junk, junk, condolences, bill, all unopened, and a mysterious plain envelope addressed to her, Lily Neff. She stared at it, almost expecting the name typed above the address to change. She never got mail.

Lily tugged the envelope out of the pile as gently as if she were playing a game of pick-up-sticks. Her heart buzzed with curiosity as she slid her finger under the envelope's flap, ripped it open, and pulled out a letter. The tower of excitement building in her chest collapsed.

She tossed the form letter into the recycling and wondered how she got on that mailing list. Surely credit card companies weren't supposed to solicit eleven-year-olds.

"Would you like a snack?" she asked herself, forcing the cheer back into her voice, and opened the fridge to see the options. She deliberately did not glance at the freezer.

Before Lily's twin, Anders, got sick, the last day of school—which he called the first afternoon of summer—meant popsicles. Lily always had strawberry and Anders chose orange or lime, and they ate them outside, sitting on the cover of the old well, even if it was chilly or raining. Anders, who loved traditions almost as much as he loved plans, never forgot to put *popsicles* on the shopping list, and never let Lily open the box before the first afternoon of summer began.

If Anders hadn't gotten sick, they'd be eating popsicles in the sunshine right now. Anders would taste his slowly, while Lily went in for the chomp. They'd argue out plans for the weeks ahead, and Anders would laugh and call Lily "big beaver" when she gnawed the wooden popsicle stick until it splintered. If Anders hadn't gotten sick, there would be picnics on the dock and baseball on the radio, and bug bites and sunburns and badminton and movie nights. A whole perfect summer would stretch before them.

But Anders had gotten sick. He'd gotten sick and he had died, and everything was different. Lily still had big plans for the summer, but she'd be hatching her schemes close to home—and keeping them top secret.

Lily spotted a promising-looking baking dish in the middle of the fridge, and peeked beneath its tinfoil. Sure enough, Connie Heanssler, who lived up the road a piece, had dropped off another lasagna. Lily pulled it out and helped herself, eating directly from the pan.

"Mmm," she said, because it was good, and because ever since Anders got sick, she'd made a point of having a healthy appetite, one fit for a healthy, growing girl. At first she'd done it so Anders and Mom wouldn't worry about her being sick too, but even once it was clear she couldn't feed Anders by eating enough for them both, and that Mom had stopped noticing what, when, or whether Lily ate at all, it still felt important to prove she was okay.

She lifted a third, fourth, fifth cheesy forkful to her mouth, and gazed out the window as she chewed. Outside, several cars drove by, probably faster than they should. One honked at a short-haired teenager going the opposite way on her bike.

Quinn, the girl's name was. Lily recognized her, as she did most kids within a few years of her own age. This was a small, rural community, the kind of place where everyone knew everything about everyone else, or thought they did. And with kindergartners through seventh graders all at one school, and grades eight through twelve at the other, you encountered most people eventually. Quinn hadn't been at Lily's school this year though. She'd just finished her first year of high school. Lily wondered a million things about what that was like.

Quinn's T-shirt billowed behind her and she glanced

at Lily's house as she pedaled past. Something familiar but new lurched in Lily's gut: fear. She swallowed hard.

If she could move at impossible speeds—in a zippy blur, like Sonic the Hedgehog—she would scribble a sign that said *YOU SHOULD WEAR A HELMET* and press it to the window to warn Quinn of the terrible things that could happen. But of course she couldn't do that. Not before the teenager flew out of sight.

Sure enough, seconds later, Quinn crested the hill and was gone. Lily pictured her coasting toward the pond with the wind in her hair—soaring down the long hill for that glorious moment before she'd have to pedal her butt off to get up the next one.

Lily and Anders weren't allowed to bike on these hills, even with helmets on. People drove too fast and the road was too narrow, Mom said. Instead, they rode up and down the dirt driveway or, when they tired of that, through the bumpy, grassy field.

Lily imagined Quinn getting wherever she was going safely, and assured herself it would be okay.

When she'd shoveled down all the lasagna she could fit, she put the rest in the fridge and went to hunt for her sweatshirt. It was warm out now in the afternoon sun, but evenings in Maine cooled off fast, and Lily knew she'd want to stay outside as long as possible. She rescued the sweatshirt from where it had dropped behind the couch, and froze.

The door between the living room and sewing room was closed, but Lily could hear her mother behind it. Not sewing—Mom almost never worked during normal hours anymore. Her sewing machine whirred in the middle of the night, when most people were sleeping. Mom was talking in what Lily recognized as her phone voice—a little louder and more exaggerated than how she'd speak to someone in the same room.

Lily crept closer and put one eye to the crack between the wall and the door, but it wasn't wide enough for peeking. "Uh-huh," she heard. "He did?" *Pause.* "That's just like him. He always loved animals. All critters, even spiders and snakes. He was gentle and kind with them, ever since he was a baby."

Mom was crying a little, Lily could tell, but she also sounded happy, in a dreamy-removed way. Lily balled her hands into fists so tight her fingernails bit her palms. She squeezed harder.

"I love knowing he and Barkly are together," Mom said, sniffling. "I'm glad he isn't lonely without us."

Lily didn't have to ask—she knew who Mom was talking to.

Lorelei, the psychic medium, who claimed to have a special gift that meant she could communicate with the dead.

Lorelei the total fake. The utter fraud. The fifty-dollar-an-hour *liar*.

Lily had never met Lorelei or heard her voice. She didn't even know what the woman looked like—if she used a crystal ball and wore long earrings and scarves like Lily pictured, or if those were just for psychics in movies—but she hated her. She hated all the lies the psychic told about Anders, and how desperately Mom gobbled them up. She hated how their calls kept Mom floating outside of reality.

"Did he say anything about Mimi?" Mom asked.

Lily huffed her annoyance. She couldn't tell Mom the psychic was fake. She couldn't explain how she knew. Hearing the truth would only upset Mom, and besides, Mom wouldn't believe her. Lily's secret was impossible to share.

Luckily there was someone else who understood exactly how Lily felt. She tied the sweatshirt around her waist and ran outside to find him.

3

A Secret Spot

The tire swing on the apple tree was only just around the back of the large red barn—tucked behind the brambles at the edge of the field, where the woods began—but it had always seemed to Lily like a secret, separate pocket of the world. If she stood on the tire swing, holding on to the ropes for balance, she could see past the tops of the spruce trees, down the hill, to the cattail-fringed pond and the road behind it. If she spun the other way, careful not to pinch her hands in the twisting ropes, the whole field stretched before her, too far to shout, way out to where the woods wrapped around it. If she reclined on the swing and let her hair skim the grass, endless sky flew above her.

A person would have to be looking hard to find anyone

in this spot, which made it perfect for her and Anders—both when he'd been alive and when he wasn't.

Lily didn't see her twin as she approached their tire swing on the first afternoon of summer, but when she reached it, there he was. "Hey," he said.

"Hey," she said, and plopped onto the ground beside him. The tangle in her chest unraveled quickly, but not before Anders sensed it.

He glanced at her sideways. "What?" he asked.

Lily tilted her face toward the blue of the sky, closed her eyes, and felt a breeze kiss her eyelids. The first afternoon of summer was downright showing off. "Nothing," she said. "Just Mom stuff."

He nodded. She didn't have to explain. He picked a long, wide blade of grass, pinned it flat between his thumbs, moved his hands to his lips, and blew. Lily grinned at the balloon-bird squeal it produced.

She reached for a blade of her own, positioned it like he'd done, and blew as hard as she could. Instead of a squeal, it made an enormous fart.

Anders burst out laughing and Lily tried again, but with her brother cracking up beside her, which cracked *her* up as she exhaled, her second attempt was more spatter than whistle. "Hold on, I've almost got it," she said. She cupped her hands to her mouth, inhaled dramatically, and released the grossest, loudest, wettest noise she could make, without even trying to vibrate the grass.

Anders fell over, and Lily tossed the blade aside with a smirk. Making him laugh was so satisfying.

"You should try out for band," he said when he'd recovered. "You've got to share that talent with the world."

"But is the fart hand a percussion instrument or a horn?" She pictured herself tooting away in a stiff polyester uniform, ending each song with a blast.

"It's a wind instrument. Duh."

"Oh, right. Like 'breaking wind,'" she said.

He rolled his eyes like that joke was too obvious. Mischief spread across his face. "Can you imagine what Ms. Lambert would do if you really tried to audition like that? I would pay a hundred bucks to see it."

She pressed her palm to her lips. "*Pffffffffft.*"

Anders applauded high in the air. "Bravo! Encore, encore!"

Lily stood and gave a deep bow, with a sweep of her arms at the finish. She twirled, landed on the swing, and kicked off. Nothing felt more summery than soaring. Leaning back, she imagined this was the only moment that existed.

When she came back down, her feet hit the ground with a thud. "Hey," she said, keeping her toes anchored while the swing twisted. "You haven't seen Barkly, have you?" She knew the answer but had to check.

Anders blinked. "Who?"

"Never mind." She twisted away, and the swing spun back again. The green spruce and gray apple tree blurred in her vision.

He scrunched his nose. "Barkly the dog? From when Mom was little?" She nodded. Their mom kept a photo of the shaggy, happy dog on her dresser, yet had never budged when her children begged, campaigned, or argued to please please please adopt a dog of their own. A dog, she said, would be too much nuisance. "Why would I— Oh." His shoulders drooped. "Mom talked to the psychic again."

"Yup," Lily confirmed.

"Ugh." Everything the psychic said annoyed Anders too, but not for the same reason. He got frustrated because he felt misunderstood. He hated when people put words in his mouth, especially if they were the wrong words. The only one he let speak for him was Lily, and that was different. When Lily spoke for Anders, she was speaking for them both.

An idea bubbled inside her like soda fizzing up a glass. "Okay, but what if you *did* talk to Lorelei? Like, we could make up a bunch of outrageous stuff and you'd pass it along just to mess with her. Wouldn't that be great?"

Anders shook his head slightly, the way he did when she made a doomed move in Othello. "That's not messing with her. It's making her legit. If I did that, she really would be communicating with the dead."

Lily's bubbles went flat. "Oh. That's true. I forgot."

"Anyway, it wouldn't work." He nudged the tire with his foot and she swayed. "You're the only one I can talk to. Sorry, Barkly."

"Aw, you're still a good girl, Barkly." Lily petted an imaginary dog in the space between them. Anders scratched Barkly's invisible ears, and ducked away from a face lick. Lily giggled.

"Hey, wanna work on our squirrel fort?" Anders asked. "I bet we could weave these longer grasses into a welcome mat. And we should make them a little squirrel broom."

"Yeah!" she said, and kneeled beside him to pick the longest stalks.

Of course he wasn't lonely in the afterlife. He still, like always, had Lily.

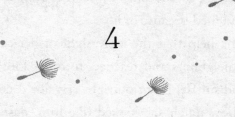

4

Before and After

After Anders died, adults said things like "He went so quickly" and "It was just so sudden." But to Lily, the months when her brother was sick had lasted an eternity. Each minute was like a piece of gum pinched and stretched so thin that it almost broke, or almost broke her, until it looped back around to be chewed and pulled again, hour after hour, day after day, with all the flavor gnawed out of it. By the time it was over and Anders was gone, time was broken. It never moved like it had before.

Then again, nothing was like it had been before—including Lily. Anders had always been part of who she was. Lily wasn't Lily without him.

She felt like a ghost. An extremely angry ghost. A ghost

who had failed at the only thing that mattered, and her brother had died because of it.

It didn't help that the mere sight of her caused everyone from neighbors and teachers to other kids' parents to tear up and sniffle, if not outright cry. She'd never been so aware of how much she looked like him, despite his long face and her round one, his scrawny arms and her muscles, his well-behaved hair that grew straight to his chin and her unruly waves all over the place. When people looked at her, they saw his absence.

She felt it constantly too. It was a deep, horrible ache that wanted to rage to the surface.

Lily hated the weeping. What right did anyone else have to cry? Lily wasn't crying, and she was the one who had lost her twin. She was the one who would miss him forever.

She missed him the way she would miss her own arm if it upped and disappeared. She kept reaching for things and remaining empty-handed. She kept needing her brother and finding he wasn't there.

If Anders didn't exist, how could Lily? *Why* should Lily?

She couldn't. She didn't.

Yet somehow, there she was. A girl-shaped void. A sudden abyss. She folded herself into his absence until she took up negative space.

For three full days, Lily floated through time without him, grounded to nothing, completely numb.

On the third day, after his funeral, their house filled up with visitors, casseroles, and grief. She slipped outside and ran to the tire swing. There she found him, waiting. Swinging.

She hadn't exactly known he would be there, but she wasn't completely surprised either. It made more sense than his *not* being there. And he didn't treat it like a big deal.

"Want a turn?" he'd asked, and leaped off the swing, landing with his usual grace. Landing in the dead, brown grass. The grass that would soon turn green.

Lily accepted the tire swing. She pushed off from the ground, pumped her legs, felt the wind, and slowly came back to life.

She closed her eyes, breathed in deep, and exhaled, soaring forward. When she opened them, Anders was still there.

She stuck out her tongue. "Thanks for abandoning me," she said.

He blushed, and stuck his tongue out too. "Not by choice," he said.

She'd have expected a hallucination or apparition to shimmer a little, or be translucent, or at least seem kind of blurry at the edges. But Anders was solidly Anders. He looked like himself: real and present and hers.

Still, she didn't dare try to touch him.

"Apology accepted," she said, because they never stayed mad, and because dying wasn't really his fault.

"How long has it been?" he asked.

She stopped the swing. "Three days."

He nodded. She waited for him to say more, but he didn't. She wasn't sure how much he remembered about the infection or the seizure or the ambulance or the end. He hadn't been fully conscious for all of it. But Lily had. She would never forget.

"Did it hurt?" she asked.

He looked surprised. "What, dying?"

"Yeah."

He paused. "I don't know."

"What do you mean you don't know?"

Anders gave the kind of shrug most people assumed meant he was finished talking, but which Lily knew meant he needed space to think with less pressure. She shooed her impatience and it scurried away.

Anders squinted at the clouds, then at his sister, like he was trying to bring her face into focus, or maybe see through something hazy right in front of it. She kept still. "That's not how it works," he said finally. "It's not what matters anymore."

She held in a sigh of frustration. He was reaching the end of his words, but she needed him to explain. Nothing about his dying made any sense, except for the fact that he'd come back to her. Nothing about it seemed at all fair. "What does matter?" she asked.

He frowned. "Potatoes," he declared.

Her heart skipped with surprise. "What?"

"Potatoes!" he repeated. His expression stayed serious, but she knew he was goofing around. It was his favorite way of changing the subject.

She gave in. He would only clam up if she pushed.

"You're such a spud face," she said.

He crossed his arms. "Don't be a tater hater."

She huffed and twirled on the swing. "Whatever, spuddles."

"Takes one to know one," he shot back, and Lily smiled for the first time in days. He grinned, victorious. "Potato pants."

"Your turn," she said, and slid off the tire. He didn't move to take it. "Or do you want to go do something else? The house is full of people, but we could hang out in the barn. Or spy in the tree house. Or be baby wolf cubs lost in the woods."

He shook his head. "I can't."

Panic shot up her spine and whooshed through her thoughts. She'd only just gotten her brother back—she wasn't ready for him to go. She opened her mouth to protest, but Anders spoke first.

"I mean, I can't go other places. Right here is the only overlap."

"Overlap?" Lily echoed.

"Yeah." He searched for words to explain. "It's not like this anymore, anywhere else. For me. It's only like this here. Only with you."

"This is the spot where we overlap," she said, and he looked relieved she understood. "It's an Us Thing," she added.

"An Us Thing," he confirmed, and settled onto the grass.

Lily sat beside him and shivered. The ground was lumpy and cold, still half frozen. Anders didn't seem to notice. She wished she had grabbed a warmer jacket.

She wrapped her arms around her knees for warmth. "So are you haunting me?" she asked.

He snorted. "You wish."

"*Ooooo-eeeeee-ooooh*," she wailed in her spookiest voice. He tossed a handful of grass at her face. She ducked.

"How's Mom?" he asked.

"Really sad," she said. She looked down. "Too sad for *sad* to describe it. I wish she could see you."

He grimaced. "I wish so too."

"Can you stay?" Lily blurted. "I mean, can we meet here again? In the overlap? Tomorrow?"

"I don't know," he said. "I hope so. I'll try."

"Okay," she said. "Me too."

A slow smile spread on her face. "We're sailors on a ship

in the middle of the ocean and a terrible storm's approaching," she said.

He jumped to his feet. "Lower the sails and batten down the hatches," he shouted. "And hold on tight! There are sharks in these waters."

"And sea monsters!"

They played in the overlap until he disappeared at dusk, and she worried she might have imagined it. Even in her own head, it sounded impossible: *He came back*. But she felt better in a way only being with Anders could bring.

That was an Us Thing too.

5

What Is and Is Not an Us Thing

Lily couldn't remember the first Us Thing she and Anders shared. It probably happened in the womb or their cradles. Her whole life was full of things only the two of them understood.

Like how hearing the word *plumber* made them burst into giggles, though they couldn't explain why (and if anyone asked, it made them laugh harder). Or the way Lily could often tell what Anders was thinking without him saying a single word—and he sometimes knew what she was feeling before she'd realized it herself.

Their solemn belief that fluffernutter sandwiches tasted best cut in quarters, diagonally. Their love for the scent of old books, especially the bindings, and especially the Stonington Public Library's Beverly Cleary collection. (Lily's favorite book to sniff was *Dear Mr. Henshaw*, but Anders thought *Ramona Forever* smelled nicest.) Their agreement that dressing alike in homemade outfits for holiday photos was silly, but they would never, ever tell Mom, since she would pretend she was okay with them stopping. How no one made Lily laugh harder than Anders, and no one could make her more furious either, sometimes in back-to-back moments.

All of those were Us Things. In some ways, her whole life was one.

They didn't share a brain or have ESP, like some people thought was clever to ask. But she and Anders had been a unit since before they were born. They'd spent more time together than they'd ever spent apart, and with all that practice observing him, she'd become an Anders expert. He was an expert on her too.

No one else she'd met knew what it was like to be a twin raised on an island by a single mom—*their* mom, who might forget about bedtime because she was so wrapped up in gluing sequins onto enormous, fluttery butterfly wings or baking spur-of-the-moment brownies, but who never forgot that Anders liked eating the brownies' crispy corners while Lily preferred the gooey middle. No one else got that it was normal and not especially interesting to come from a sperm donor, not a dad, and be related to only the people you lived with—no aunts, cousins, or grandparents. She didn't have to explain to Anders how the salt-pine-granite air and the field, pond, ocean, and woods were as much a part of who she was as her kidneys, opinions, and dreams—even if neighbors considered her "from away" since her grandparents and great-grandparents weren't born here. He knew the ways it felt when most of your classmates were cousins, third cousins, or second cousins twice removed, and you weren't included in any of that—but you had a twin who was totally yours, which more than made up for it.

But what it was like to lose your twin and suddenly *not* have that? That wasn't an Us Thing. Only Lily knew how that felt.

She'd described it to him as best she could: how when she went back to school twelve days after he died, she wasn't so much *in* school as haunting it. She drifted through her old routine, amazed that it used to matter. Jarred by everyone and everything that went on as before but without him. It was impossible not to resent it all.

Drastic measures were required to keep herself from breaking down.

As she went through the motions in class after class, she kept to herself and refused eye contact. She looked only at the teacher, the whiteboard, and her desk. She blocked out everything else.

Her classmates took the hint. They ignored her so

completely, she almost believed she wasn't there. But she wasn't invisible—quite the opposite.

She was an ant under a magnifying glass. A girl inside a bubble. A radioactive freak no one came within six feet of.

(Anders had liked that description best. "You sound like a superhero. Do radioactive freaks get special powers?"

She gave him a pointed look. "You mean besides seeing ghosts?"

His laugh made everything better.)

The one person who tried to approach her on the playground, or looked for a second like she might, Lily had glared at and pivoted to avoid. She hadn't forgiven a word of what Deandra had said in their fight three weeks before. Lily wasn't about to be her friend again just because Anders was gone. She would rather be alone than have company like that.

But she didn't tell Anders that part. Deandra wasn't worth explaining.

And Lily wasn't alone. She had Anders in the overlap. She didn't need anyone else.

When she was with him, she was herself again. But everywhere else, she was a pant: a pair of jeans sliced in half—one leg and half a butt, flopping around. Useless.

Jeans, khakis, overalls, corduroys—pants were always plural. Without Anders, she was basically a rag.

Anders listened and looked sympathetic to this rant,

but Lily knew he didn't fully get it. How could he? It was impossible for her to show him what things were like for her without him.

She knew because he couldn't show her who he was without her, either. She'd spent nearly three whole months hanging out with her dead brother, and she didn't really know what being dead was like.

That wasn't an Us Thing either, and Lily hated it.

6

Double Trouble

The first full day of summer started early and bright, with a black-throated green warbler serving as Lily's alarm clock. Before it reached the last note of its high-pitched song, she was wide awake and eager to get moving. She wanted to check if any bushy red squirrels with black stripes down their sides had discovered the new additions to the squirrel fort.

The tiny broom Anders had made out of a stick, a string, and some straw had turned out perfectly, and he'd found a leaf to go with it that was curled on one end so the squirrels could use it as a dustpan. The welcome mat Lily had woven from grass was slightly lumpy and a little misshapen, but Anders had assured her the squirrels would still love it.

They hadn't seen any red squirrels actually using the fort, but it had only existed for a week, and there was still lots of building and decorating to do. The plan for today was to make pillows for the mossy beds and find acorns to put in the kitchen. Anders also wanted to reinforce the south wall with additional twigs and mud, and they'd been debating whether and where to add a swimming pool. Lily wasn't sure whether squirrels liked to swim. Anders argued they might if they had a waterslide.

Lily dressed quickly, brushed her teeth, and peeked around the corner into Mom's room. Mom was curled up in bed, facing away from the door, with her long, dark hair across the pillow. A few silver strands gleamed in the light streaming in through the open window. They reminded Lily of tinsel. From the way the lump of blankets rose and fell in a steady rhythm, Lily guessed Mom was sleeping. She tiptoed away from the door to let her rest.

In the kitchen, Lily danced around in her sneakers while she waited for breakfast to pop. When the toast was done, she smeared it with crunchy peanut butter and ate it on her way to the overlap. As she'd expected, Anders wasn't there yet.

She swallowed the last bite of toast and licked the drips of melted peanut butter off her fingers. They were a sticky mess. She wiped her hands on the back of her shorts and bent to peek at the squirrel fort under the spruce tree.

"Shouldn't you wipe your butt *before* leaving the house?" Anders said. His voice made her jump.

She whirled around, preparing a comeback, but as soon as she saw him, her jaw dropped and her snappy retort was forgotten. She stared in disbelief.

Anders was dressed in the exact same outfit as Lily, from the sparkling butterflies on his tank top right down to his rainbow socks. He even had a small stain on the cuff of his turquoise shorts. Only his face didn't mirror hers. He looked exceedingly pleased with himself.

"Copycat. How did you know what I'd be wearing?" she demanded.

He put his hands on his hips and jutted his chin. "How did *you* know what *I'd* be wearing?" he said.

A snort erupted out of her nostrils at the same time one escaped his. "You're ridiculous," she said.

"Thank you." His lips twitched. Hers twitched back. "You're lucky I didn't put googly eyes on your toothbrush and short-sheet your bed."

Lily shook her head. "What are you talking about, dinglenut?"

"Isn't it April Fools' Day?" he asked. He looked down at his colorful outfit.

"No! It's June!"

He grinned like he'd known that all along.

Lily looked at her silly look-alike twin and laughed so hard her side hurt. He collapsed on the grass beside her. The giggles turned their faces bright red.

"Lily?" Mom's voice came suddenly, like a hiccup, and snapped Lily out of her glee. Mom was already inside the overlap. Lily hadn't even heard her approach. "Are you okay?" Mom asked.

Lily's heart beat fast, and, for one confused second, she worried she and Anders would get in trouble.

With a whoosh of sadness, she realized they couldn't.

She glanced at the spot where Anders had been, but her brother was nowhere to be seen.

Of course. With Mom here, this wasn't the overlap. It was just the edge of the field and the woods, and a tire swing, and Lily on the ground, no longer laughing.

She sat up. "I'm okay," she said. She couldn't say what she'd been doing or explain what had been so funny. It would sound like a lie. A delirious lie. And Mom already looked dazed and worried.

Mom's eyes flitted in all directions. "I thought I heard something," she said.

Lily gazed up at Mom, who stood barefoot in crumpled pajamas, looking around for something that wasn't there, and felt a rush of hope.

Maybe Mom had heard him laughing.

Maybe the breeze carried his voice through Mom's bedroom window, and she already knew he'd been there.

Maybe sensing him had pulled her out of bed and brought her toward them.

Maybe all Lily had to do was tell her, and Mom would know and believe it was true.

"What did you hear?" Lily asked. Her voice pitched high with exhilaration.

Mom blinked. "I'm not sure. Some kind of crash. Metal on metal. A car? Except it wasn't. I don't know. You didn't hear it? It woke me up."

Lily's hope sank. "I didn't hear it."

Mom looked at her hands as though she wasn't sure where they had come from. "I guess it was in my dream," she said. Her arms dropped to her sides. "That's a relief." She sounded exhausted.

Lily fumbled to her feet. "You want breakfast?" she asked. "I'll make toast. Toast and an egg if you'd like one. Or some tea?"

Mom smiled weakly. "No, thanks. Did you eat?" Lily nodded. "Good. It's such a nice day. I'm glad you're outside." Mom squinted at the sky, and her eyes filled with tears. "A full blue day," she said, which was what Anders would have called it.

"Yeah," Lily said. Mom turned to go, and Lily swallowed the word *stay*.

When Mom drifted into her cloud of grief, Lily couldn't follow.

7

Measuring Time and Space

When Anders was alive, Mom often joked that he operated in his own time zone, Anders Standard Time, which moved at an unpredictable pace. He'd lose whole hours or afternoons to daydreams, take a nap right after breakfast, be wide awake with ideas at midnight, get excited for sledding in summer. He didn't so much lose track of time as live outside it. It often fell to Lily to be his clock.

Anders, not alive, was even worse. He never knew what day or time it was, how long it had been since he'd last appeared, or when he might show up next.

At first, Lily tried to set a schedule. "Meet me after breakfast?" she'd say. Or, "I'll come after school tomorrow." Anders would agree, then show up or not, and for Lily, that got frustrating. The first time, she freaked out, thinking it meant he was gone for good. She'd stood in the overlap, completely alone, and almost, *almost* cried, which she hadn't done since Anders got sick—not even at his funeral. Instead, she kicked a tree, hurting her toes and startling a field mouse who'd been searching for food nearby. When Anders arrived a minute later, he found her hopping on one foot, her cheeks red and splotchy, apologizing to the tree, which didn't appear to have minded.

"Now you're on Anders *Un*standard Time," she said at the end of March, when he had been dead fourteen days and shown up late for the second time.

"Not even." Anders tilted the dried leaf he was holding, considering it. "I don't feel any time at all."

"Like, it's stopped moving?" she asked.

"More like it's stopped *being*. There is no time, except the time I spend with you." He pinched the maple leaf's edges. Little bits of it fell away.

"Huh." Lily couldn't quite imagine that. She felt every rigid second that passed without him. Time only relaxed and unfurled when they were together. "But you exist when you're not with me, right?"

"Sure." He held up the leaf, now shaped like a star, and placed it on a branch of the apple tree. "It's just different. There's no overlap and no time. No plumbers."

The leaf fell and twirled like a whirligig. Lily's stomach

spun too. She didn't laugh. "What's here when the overlap's not?" She pictured him wandering in darkness, through a whole lot of empty, awful nothing.

He shrugged. "I don't know. When it's here, it's here. When it isn't, it isn't. Same as me, I guess."

"But . . ." Lily wanted to object, though she wasn't sure to what, or why she was arguing. Maybe it just felt good to quarrel with him again.

"Do you ever come here without me?" she asked. She selected a leaf of her own and tried to tear it into a crescent— a moon to go with his star—but it was much harder than he'd made it look. The leaf was brittle and fragile after all those months of winter, and it didn't want to be crescent shaped. It disintegrated under her touch. She put her hands back in her pockets. The day was sunny but still cold. It would be another week before crocuses came up—the first squat, purple flowers of spring. But the ground had started to thaw, and Lily's sneakers were muddy around the edges.

"Nope. I think I'm only here because of you," he said.

"Like, I summon you?"

"No, dingus. I'm not your genie in a bottle."

"More like magnets?" She liked that idea of them, as opposite poles always pulled together by an invisible current between them.

But Anders looked annoyed. "I don't know. I'm not a

scientist, okay? I don't have any more answers about this than you do."

"Okay," she said. He relaxed. "But we should figure it out. The parts we can. We should see where the borders of the overlap are, and mark them."

He tensed back up. "Why?"

"I want to know! It's not fair you can see them and I can't."

He'd given in, as Lily knew he would. Slowly, he walked along the perimeter of where he could be, while Lily placed branches and rocks to mark the boundaries. It didn't change anything, of course, but it felt good to collect information.

Anders absolutely refused, however, to see what would happen if he stepped beyond the periphery or reached a hand across it. "Just a finger?" Lily suggested, which was one push too far, and for the next several minutes he was quiet and sulky, not even seeming to care what the Red Sox's starting lineup would be, or the other stuff she'd read about baseball's opening day.

He got over being mad, as he always did. He'd never gotten good at holding grudges, since Lily always held them for him. And the next day, when she brought a radio so they could listen to the first pitch together, he'd seemed pleased. But when they discovered the reception was all static in the overlap, he just shrugged. Only Lily was truly disappointed.

They acted out and announced their own imaginary

game, with Lily giving the play-by-play and Anders as the color commentator, until the sky turned to sherbet as the sun ducked behind the trees, and she went inside to hear the last few innings with Mom, who only half listened.

The overlap always faded at dusk.

But now, in mid-June, the sun rose early and lingered well past dinner, taking its nice slow time making its way across the sky, seeming to want each day to last, just like Lily did. When she arrived at the overlap on the fourth full day of summer, she didn't even mind that Anders was late. She pulled a book from her backpack, climbed into the apple tree, and settled against the V of its trunk.

Two and a half chapters in, she glanced up as she turned a page, and something caught her eye. It was that teenager, Quinn, the one she'd seen biking past her house on the last day of school, and yesterday during breakfast too. Quinn wasn't on her bike now though. She stood at the edge of the pond down the hill, holding one end of a stick.

Lily watched, curious, as Quinn maneuvered the long stick through the murky brown water. It looked like she was stirring it.

Lily frowned. She plucked a leaf to use as a bookmark and jumped down from the apple tree. She hadn't thought to bring binoculars to the overlap, so she would have to go down there to investigate. She hoped Quinn wasn't disturbing the frogs.

She walked, then ran, down the steep hill toward Quinn—momentum pushing her faster, faster, closer, closer—and as the ground evened out below her feet, she saw it wasn't a stick Quinn held after all. It was a pole. Quinn stirred again and lifted the pole from the water. Lily slowed her steps. On one end of Quinn's pole was a net. The teenager was fishing for something.

"Hey," Lily called from a few yards away. She didn't think Quinn had noticed her yet and she didn't want to startle her.

Quinn lifted her chin. "Hey," she said, and returned her focus to fishing.

Lily closed the distance between them cautiously. Quinn was unexpectedly tall up close.

Quinn dipped the net in the pond. "What are you catching?" Lily asked after a few seconds of watching.

"Garbage," Quinn said. She swooped the pole to one side and lifted it, forcing Lily to jump out of the way. Quinn tilted the pole to empty the net, and a clear plastic cup fell to the ground. "Jerk," she muttered.

Lily felt a jolt of shock. She immediately regretted coming down here. "Sorry," she said, backing away from the surly teenager. "I didn't mean to—"

"What?" Quinn squinted at her, as if seeing her for the first time. Lily tried to look as harmless as possible. "No, not you," Quinn said. "I mean, unless you're the jerk who tossed this cup in here."

"I'm definitely not." Lily shook her head to emphasize her innocence.

Quinn's lips quirked. "I didn't think so." She turned and plunged her net back into the pond. Lily moved to Quinn's other side to avoid being in her way again.

Quinn leaned dangerously close to the water and scooped up a lid and straw. "Gotcha," she said, and deposited them next to the plastic cup. Lily wished she had a pole and net too. Fishing for garbage looked fun.

"What are you going to do with it?" she asked.

"Throw it away," Quinn said, in a tone that suggested that was obvious. "Or recycle it, if it's recyclable. Like whoever chucked it out their window should have done in the first place."

"Oh," Lily said. "That's nice of you."

The teenager shrugged. "I just don't get it. Who drives all the way back from Dunkin'—that's, like, thirty minutes away, right? At least. So you've definitely finished your iced coffee or whatever before you get to the island. And instead of waiting until you're home and can throw it out like a civilized person, you decide to roll down your window and toss it into a pond? Who *does* that? We all have to live here. Who do they think is going to clean it up?"

"The garbage fairy?" Lily suggested.

Quinn smirked. "Ah, yes. That's me. The tooth fairy's lesser-known cousin." Lily giggled. Quinn sighed. "Twinkle twinkle," she said, and sank the net into the water once more.

Out of the corner of her eye, Lily saw a flash of movement, and the telltale splash that followed confirmed it was a frog jumping out of the way. But she was no longer worried about the frogs. Obviously, Quinn's fishing for garbage was good for them.

Lily wanted to stay and talk with Quinn longer, but she also wanted to go find Anders and tell him how she'd made the prickly teenager smile. And she definitely didn't want Quinn to think she was hanging around too long and getting pesky. But she felt brave enough to push her luck on one thing. "Hey, I wanted to tell you," she said, before she could lose her nerve. "You really should wear a helmet when you're biking. Especially on this road."

Quinn blinked. "What are you, the island safety patrol?" she asked.

Lily lifted and dropped one shoulder. "I just don't want to have to use that net to scoop your brains off the pavement, that's all."

Quinn let out a surprised laugh. "That's dark," she said, and nodded slowly, approvingly. "I like you."

Lily glowed under the strange compliment.

"All right," Quinn said. "I'll try to remember next time. I do have one; I just sometimes forget."

"Oh!" Lily said, sounding more eager than she meant to. "Cool! I mean, that's great! Thanks!" Amusement spread across Quinn's face, and Lily's own smile felt bigger than it had in ages. If she stood there any longer, she'd start bouncing. "Gotta go!"

She turned and ran up the hill toward the overlap before Quinn could take back her promise.

8

The Mystery of Quinn

The next morning, instead of bringing her blackberry jam on toast outside to eat while she waited for Anders, Lily stood by the window and nibbled slowly, watching the road for Quinn. She didn't know for certain that Quinn would bike past, but if she did, Lily wanted to see it. There weren't many other kids who lived within walking or biking distance from her house, and there weren't any besides Quinn who'd already graduated from preschool, so of course Lily was curious about her. But she wasn't watching to be nosy. She only wanted to know if Quinn had remembered the helmet.

After the last bite of toast was gone, she made a game of drinking her orange juice with the tiniest sips possible—like she was a hummingbird feeding on droplets of nectar pulled from a bright orange flower. It took a full eight minutes to empty the small glass and get all the little bits of pulp stuck to its sides. A real hummingbird probably would have been much faster.

Still no Quinn.

She was about to give up when the teenager pedaled into sight. Lily leaned forward, almost pressing her face to the window screen. Quinn's purple helmet glinted in the sun before she passed out of view without glancing in Lily's direction. Lily's heart thrummed, triumphant. She ran outside to tell Anders.

"Is she down at the pond now?" he asked, even though he was the one standing on the tire swing. He couldn't see anything outside the overlap.

They traded places and Lily checked. "Nope," she said, and swooped back and forth through the air a few times before jumping off to forfeit the swing.

"So where does she go every day?" he wondered, which of course made her wonder too.

"I don't know. Maybe she fishes for garbage in other ponds," she said, only half kidding. Quinn had seemed pretty passionate about cleaning up litter. Lily thought that was cool.

"Was she carrying the net on her bike today?" he asked. She thought for a second and shook her head. "Then no," he decided. He perked up. "Maybe there's a secret hangout where high schoolers go in the summer. Like how in movies they go to malls and Starbucks and concerts and stuff."

Lily scrunched up her nose, thinking. "I doubt it. She'd have to bike to, like, Bangor for that. It would take all day. But maybe she goes to a friend's house or something."

"And stops on the way to fish for garbage?"

Lily shrugged. "I guess so. Who can say? Teenagers are very mysterious."

"But interesting," Anders said. Lily agreed.

The next day, she didn't see any sign of Quinn during breakfast, but when she stepped outside to go to the overlap, the crunch of tires on gravel beckoned her attention. She turned to look, and there was Quinn—not only wearing the purple helmet, but biking up Lily's driveway. Quinn waved and rolled to a stop in front of the barn doors.

"There you are," Quinn said, as if she'd been searching for Lily everywhere. "Are you ready to go meet some chickens?"

"Meet chickens?" Lily echoed. She wasn't sure if that was a joke, like *Why did the chicken cross the road?*, but if it was, she was missing the punch line.

"Yeah," Quinn said, as though it made perfect sense. "Candy Turner's chickens. You know her?" Lily did. Ms. Turner lived up the next hill. Lily hadn't known about the chickens though. "I said I'd feed them. Thought you might want to help out," Quinn explained.

"Okay," Lily said. She still didn't really understand what Quinn was asking *her* for, but she didn't need to know to say yes. She slipped off her backpack. "Let me tell my mom where I'm going," she said, and ran inside.

A minute later, they were walking in the narrow strip of gravel beside the road, Quinn wheeling her bike up ahead and Lily following a few feet behind her. There wasn't enough space to walk side by side. There was barely enough space to walk at all. When cars came, they had to step into the shrubs, vines, and grasses, in case the drivers didn't see them or have room to swerve.

"Is Ms. Turner away? Why can't she feed the chickens herself?" Lily asked as they walked past the pond. A car sped by on the opposite side, sweeping her words along with it.

"Can't hear you!" Quinn said over her shoulder. "Wait till we get there."

Lily zipped her lips for the rest of the walk, though being near Quinn made her want to yabber away, perhaps because Quinn was the only person besides Mom or Anders she had talked to in ages. Perhaps because Quinn seemed so cool and like she probably knew all sorts of stuff about everything. Lily wondered what Quinn knew about her. Neither one of them had mentioned Anders.

The second hill was long and steep, and Lily was panting by the time they reached the top and turned onto the road where Ms. Turner lived. They paused to catch their breath. Quinn's cheeks were pink and, when she took off her helmet and clipped it to her bike, her bangs were matted to her forehead with sweat. She brushed them back.

"I like your helmet," Lily said.

"You're welcome," Quinn replied. She led the way toward Ms. Turner's place, a light blue trailer with white shutters and flower boxes, which was the third house on the right side of the dirt road. Purple lupines swayed next to the driveway, and Lily wanted to ask Quinn if she'd ever read that book about the Lupine Lady, who scattered seeds up and down the coast to make the world a more beautiful place. But Quinn was crouched in Ms. Turner's driveway, calling "Here, kitty kitty" to an orange-and-white cat. The tabby finished cleaning the paw he'd been licking, stretched his back legs out one at a time, and disappeared under the trailer. Quinn stood and put her hands on her hips. "He never gives me the time of day," she said. It sounded like a trait she admired.

The screen door squeaked on its hinges and Ms. Turner poked her curly-gray-haired head out. "Quinn!" she said. "Oh, and you brought Lily. How nice of you both to come." She hobbled onto the small front porch, keeping a hand on the railing. Her bright green T-shirt featured a pink flamingo standing on one leg above the word *Florida*, and there was a clunky black medical boot strapped to her left foot. "As you can see, I've had a bit of an adventure. Came to regret that one right quick. One wrong step and just . . . *zhoop!*" She made a motion that Lily wasn't entirely sure how to interpret.

"Is it broken?" she asked.

"Just a sprain," Ms. Turner said. "But it's a real pain in the neck, I tell ya. I said to Dr. Noyes, I says, 'It won't slow me down none,' but *she* says I have to rest and stay off it a full five weeks or I'll just end up back in the boot."

"Can't have that," Quinn said.

"No, ma'am," Ms. Turner agreed. "So I appreciate you two coming to help out. They put the feed in my trunk up at the tractor supply, but I am strictly forbidden from taking it out. That's where your strong arms come in."

"We're glad to be of service." Quinn moved toward the back of the car.

"It's unlocked," Ms. Turner said, and Lily wasn't surprised. Many people on the island didn't lock their houses or cars. Some even kept their keys in the ignition. "That way, you never lose 'em and don't have to carry nothing around," Deandra's grandmother Wilda had explained when Lily asked about it. Mom always locked their doors at night, but she grew up in Boston and said old habits were hard to break.

Lily joined Quinn at the open trunk, where two forty-pound bags of chicken feed lay next to a striped towel, a screwdriver, and a roll of duct tape. "I'll get one, you get the other?" Quinn asked, and lifted the first bag without waiting for an answer.

"They go right around back there, in the metal bin next to the shed. Can't miss it," Ms. Turner said.

Lily hoisted the chicken feed out of the trunk and staggered for a second before she found her balance. The bag was as large as her torso, and heavier than Quinn had made it look. She was impressed that Ms. Turner would have carried it herself if she hadn't twisted her ankle.

She walked around to the back of the trailer and hefted her load into the open bin, next to the bag Quinn had carried. Quinn nodded once and lowered the lid. "There," she said.

Lily wiped her hands on her shirt and glanced around the backyard. The house and shed were lined with gardens brimming with flowering plants. Anders would have pestered Ms. Turner with questions until he learned the name of each one, but Lily was content to admire the tangle of colors. A half dozen chickens strutted in the grass not far from the shed, pecking the ground as they roamed. They were surprisingly big and surprisingly pretty. Lily had never thought of chickens as beautiful. Quinn clucked at them but they didn't acknowledge her.

"Do you come here every day?" Lily asked. "I've seen you biking a few times," she added, hoping the question wasn't too weird or nosy. But Quinn didn't seem to mind.

"No, just today. My mom's been assigning me chores all over the place. I do a lot at my dad's aunt's place. Linda Larrabee? You know her? She's on this road too. I've been working there a bunch. Cleaning and yardwork and listening to her tell stories while she goes through her scrapbooks."

"Like a summer job?" Lily asked. Two of the chickens, reddish-brown ones with yellow beaks and red wattles, moved closer, looking curious. She held still so she wouldn't scare them, though they seemed pretty bold.

"Kind of. But instead of cash I'm earning points. The more points I have, the more often I can borrow the car when I turn sixteen and get my driver's license. Ten points for mowing Aunt Linda's lawn. Fifteen points for picking up litter for an hour. Five points to come move these bags for Ms. Turner."

So that explained why she'd been fishing in the pond. "When do you turn sixteen?"

"November tenth. I already have my learner's permit," Quinn said like it was no big deal, but it sounded like a big deal to Lily.

"Wow." She felt suddenly self-conscious about how young she must seem. But maybe Quinn didn't mind. After all, Quinn was the one who'd invited her here.

Ms. Turner tottered around the corner and lurched toward them, wincing every time she put weight on the booted foot. Lily winced too. It didn't seem like Ms. Turner should be doing that.

"Ooof," Ms. Turner said. "You're a couple of lifesavers. Don't tell my doctor you saw me stomping around like this. She'd let me have it, for sure."

Quinn moved a plastic chair closer to Ms. Turner, who sank into it. The chickens tittered with excitement.

Ms. Turner looked at Lily. "How are you and your mom holding up?" she asked. Lily snuck a glance at Quinn to see how she'd react, but Quinn didn't react at all. Lily realized she must already know about Anders.

Of course. This was an island. Everyone knew about Anders.

"We're okay," Lily said. She didn't know how else to answer that question.

"Good," Ms. Turner said. "I've been thinking about you both. I know it's hard. Lots of prayers going up from my church group."

"Thanks," Lily said, and stared at her feet. She wished someone would swoop in and rescue her from this conversation. A second later, Quinn and a chicken did.

"Should we feed them?" Quinn asked. "The chickens? That one's about to eat Lily's shoe."

Ms. Turner chuckled and Lily yelped as one of the chickens tugged at her right shoelace. The chicken picked it up and dropped it, apparently disappointed it wasn't a worm.

"Sorry," Lily said, which was the first time she'd apologized to a chicken. The chicken clucked. Quinn smiled.

"They like you," Ms. Turner said.

"They do?" Lily said, pleased.

"Oh yes. They're usually cautious around strangers but they trusted you right away. The girls are very good judges of character."

Lily smiled at hearing them called "the girls." "Or they saw I brought their food," she said. Ms. Turner laughed and Lily felt fuller at the sound of it.

"How much should we give them?" Quinn asked. She lifted the lid of the food bin.

"Just a dite. They don't need a lot of grain in summertime. All those plants and bugs to eat, plus my table scraps in the evening. If you each throw out a good handful, that'll be plenty," Ms. Turner instructed.

Quinn opened a feed bag, and Lily scooped out the pellets in cupped hands. She scattered them in the grass, and the chickens that weren't already near her came running, full bodies on scrawny legs. Watching their many-shades-of-brown and white feathers and the silly ways they moved, she couldn't help falling a little in love.

"You don't eat them, do you?" Quinn said, and Lily's joy caught in her throat. She hadn't even considered the hens might be Ms. Turner's dinner.

"No, I keep them for eggs. And for company," Ms.

Turner said. "Us old birds, we have to stick together," she added with a chortle. Lily liked how Ms. Turner wasn't afraid to laugh at her own jokes, even in front of a tough audience like Quinn. The teenager eyed the two chickens nearest her suspiciously, as if expecting they were up to no good. The chickens paid her no mind and continued eating. Lily wondered if their feathers were as soft as they looked. She wondered if they'd ever let her pet them.

"I could come back," she offered. "To help feed them. So you won't have to move around while your ankle's healing." Chickens weren't as great as dogs, but Lily liked being around them. Just watching them made her smile. And she liked the idea of being useful.

Ms. Turner considered it for a long second. "Thank you," she said. "If you're sure you don't mind, the girls and I would love that."

"I don't mind," Lily said. "Neighbors helping neighbors." It was something she'd heard Cory Gray say when Mom thanked him for mowing their lawn last week. He was one of many people who'd been doing a lot for her and Mom these past months.

Lily wanted to be the one helping for a change. And maybe sometimes on her way to Ms. Turner's or back, she'd just happen to run into Quinn.

9

A Wasted Wish

By the time her end-of-year report card arrived, Lily had forgotten school existed. She was not thrilled to be reminded.

She'd gotten into the habit of fetching the mail on her way back from Ms. Turner's most mornings. When she reached into the mailbox and pulled out the report card, her hands still smelled like the chickens. Pearl, Henrietta, Big Bertha, Snowball, and Achoo (who was named by a three-year-old) were already comfortable enough with Lily to let her pet them, though Frankie (short for Frank-hen-stein) didn't prefer it. Frankie showed affection in other ways, like following Lily around in the yard and sometimes chasing the other chickens away from her. Lily scolded Frankie when she did that, but the ornery hen was her secret favorite.

The envelope from the school was addressed to Mom, but Lily opened it herself and frowned, seeing a note attached in Ms. Thompson's familiar handwriting. She read the note quickly as she walked to the red front door, then again more slowly in the kitchen, before stuffing it back into the envelope and leaving it on the counter.

She stomped out to the overlap and fumed while she waited.

"Uh-oh," Anders said as soon as he saw her.

"What?" she shot back. She squeezed her already-crossed arms tighter against her chest. If she squeezed hard enough, maybe her head would pop off.

Anders shrugged. "Okay, fine, don't tell me."

She flopped onto the tire swing and blew her hair from her face. "I got my report card," she said.

Anders waited.

"With a *letter*."

His eyebrows went up.

"They pity passed me," she said, and felt the thump of it in her gut. "No grades for the trimester, just *pass, pass, pass*, and a note about how I missed so much school I should technically be held back, but due to the *extenuating circumstances* they decided to advance me, and they're sure I'll catch up on what I missed."

Like having a normal fifth-grade year where your brother

doesn't die could be *caught up on*. Like seeing "pass" instead of the real grades she'd earned made anything better. Like the mess of her life could be swept under a carpet, tidied up and neatly hidden, so everyone could pretend things were fine.

She imagined all the teachers and administrators feeling pleased with how kind and generous they'd been. It made her furious.

"Ms. Thompson says she hopes I'll have a healing summer and keep up with my reading, and to please reach out if there's anything she can do." Apparently the school had left several voicemails but Mom never called them back. Mom used to bake for parent-teacher conferences, be proud of good report cards, help Lily and Anders study for quizzes, and get excited about science fairs. Those voicemails were probably still on her phone, unplayed.

"Has Ms. Thompson met you?" Anders said. "You always keep up with your reading."

"Exactly!" she raged.

"You're so caught up on reading, it makes you fall behind on everything else," he joked. But Lily wasn't ready to be cheered up yet. The reminder of all the school she had missed was also a reminder of *why*, and of her horrible failure to prevent it. She dug her fingernails into the ropes, and pictured them snapping and fraying. The swing stayed solid and steady.

The words she'd been wanting to say for months bubbled out of her. "You should have told me," she said. It tasted like swamp. She kept her gaze on the rope and didn't look at him. "We could have fixed it before it got worse."

He shrugged. "Not likely."

Not likely.

The words sat on her heart, knocking to get in. They slipped in through a crack, uninvited.

She felt empty, then hyperaware. The bright green of new leaves. The murky scent of the pond. The purple balls of wild clover, each sphere a clump of tiny blossoms, each blossom a cocoon for nectar. White airplane trails overhead. A black-capped chickadee declaring its name.

Chickadee-dee-dee-dee-dee.

Her very own brother, gone but here.

A breeze whispered across her skin. She grasped for her anger. Only a sticky film of guilt remained.

Anders leaned toward her. "Does the letter say anything about me?"

"No." She matched his grin and set up the joke. "But it mentions Saint Anders. It says the whole school misses him."

His jaw dropped in exaggerated disbelief. "The *whole school*? Even kindergartners?"

"Apparently. They miss his sweet smile and kind heart."

He beamed angelically and placed his hands beneath his chin. "What a guy."

"The most perfect boy," she agreed.

"I heard he taught birds to sing," Anders said.

"I heard double rainbows appeared when he cried."

"He pooped only daisies and roses!"

Lily snickered and scrunched up her nose. "That sounds painful."

"*Thornless* roses," he added, and sighed. "What a loss to the world."

She shook her head slowly. "I only wish we could have met him."

He gave a solemn nod. "Maybe someday, if we're very, very good, we will."

They joked about Anders' sainthood because it was funny, but Lily hated when people talked like he had been perfect. No one mentioned at the funeral how spacey and weird he could be. No one reminisced about when he was cranky, how often he lost things, or that he sometimes could be kind of rude. Anders' silly, smelly, grumpy, impatient, whiny, forgetful sides were part of who he was too, and she didn't want that erased. His imperfections didn't make him less missed or important. They made him *him*.

"Do you think people's worst and best traits are related?" she asked, watching a bee hover above the clover.

He tipped his head. "Maybe. Like what?"

"I don't know. Like how Eliza is really nosy and gets up in everyone's business, but she always wants to help whoever she can."

"Sure," he said.

"Or how Mr. Sylvester's so disorganized, but he's also spontaneous and fun."

Anders smirked. "He probably still hasn't found those lost spelling tests."

"I think his cat ate them."

"I think his desk ate them."

Lily stretched to pick a puffy dandelion that had gone white behind the swing. She held it in front of her mouth, closed her eyes, and blew.

"How 'bout how you're wicked stubborn but also loyal? That's one," Anders said as the seeds dispersed.

Her eyes flew open. "I'm not stubborn," she said. He snorted. "I'm not!"

"Oh, okay."

"I'm not!" She paused. "Maybe a little." His amusement spread. "I am loyal though," she said.

He nodded. "Two sides, one coin. Anyway, it was *your* theory."

"Well, I guess I was right."

He grinned. "Definitely only a little stubborn." She tossed the dandelion stem at him. He ducked and it bounced off his shoulder. "Did you even make a wish?" he asked.

She shook her head. She didn't believe in wishes. Not anymore.

Anders did. "You should have given it to me, then. What a waste."

"There's another one right over there."

He looked around. "Where?"

"There! In front of the birch log. You're looking right at it." She motioned toward the boundary marker.

He paused for a second. "Oh yeah. Will you get it?"

She rolled her eyes. "You're such a lazy butt."

He leaned back on the ground, limbs splayed. "You won't even help your poor dead brother?" he moaned.

Lily sighed, stood, and walked to the edge of the overlap. She picked the flower gently, and brought it to him with the seeds intact.

Anders sat up straight. "Thank you, loyal twin." He thought of a wish, and blew.

10

Going, Going, Gone

It started right after New Year's, with a cold he just couldn't kick. Lily caught the cold too, but she'd gotten over it quickly. That was her first betrayal.

The first time he blacked out, she thought it was a trick or a joke. He was feeling better, finally, or at least acted like he was, so when they woke up to snow—six inches and still falling—they'd bundled up and run outside for sledding and building a snow beast. Halfway through trudging back up the big hill, Anders breathed out "Lily," released his sled, and toppled over.

Lily giggled and approached cautiously, expecting snow to the face or some other sneak attack, but he merely blinked and stayed on his back, looking groggy and disoriented. She propped him up and he leaned on her and caught his breath while she wondered what to do.

"Are you dizzy?" she asked.

"Just light-headed," he said. "We should have had breakfast first."

She looked at him hard. "I'm okay," he insisted. "Really." So she believed him.

She retrieved their sleds and followed him to the barn, where they knocked snow from their boots and brushed off their coats. Anders' cheeks shone pink beneath his snow-covered lashes, and his eyes lit up when she suggested hot chocolate. As they walked through the mudroom that connected the barn to the house, he turned to her and said, "Can this be an Us Thing? You know Mom will overreact."

She'd agreed, though a twist in her gut argued against it.

She watched him closely that whole day and he seemed fine. He didn't have much of an appetite at lunch, but lunch was lentil soup with celery and carrots, and Anders had never liked celery, which she'd never understood, since celery only tasted like crunchiness. ("Exactly," he always said whenever they had this disagreement. "It's like eating a stick. They're just tiny trees. Nom nom nom, please pass the bamboo.") Besides, they'd already filled up on a lot of hot chocolate, first stirring in cinnamon, then nutmeg, then Marshmallow Fluff, because they were genius master chefs.

Still. She should have known.

When they were toddlers, Anders had cried whenever Lily got hurt. Mom would give them each a bandage or an ice pack, as the situation called for, plus a kiss. And every time, it worked. They both felt better.

She should have been able to feel how sick he was. She should have taken some of it on herself.

That wasn't how bodies or science or twindom worked, but Lily knew deep down she had failed him nonetheless.

She didn't know it yet on that perfect day for sledding, but she knew it a week later when he passed out at school—just crumpled and sank to the ground in front of all their classmates at recess. Lily had been with Deandra by the monkey bars when it happened, but she flew to his side so fast she almost caught him. Maybe she'd sensed it was coming.

She walked him to the nurse's office and helped him lie down on the cot, though he insisted he didn't need to. The nurse wanted to know if he'd ever passed out before, and before he could lie, Lily spilled out the truth. He glared like he might never forgive her.

Later, Dr. Noyes said the cancer was growing inside him long before any symptoms showed. Anders' bruises, exhaustion, blackouts, headaches, confusion, and shortness of breath—all the things he and Lily had been hiding—weren't even the actual problems. They were signs of something worse, something Lily couldn't have known to look for, something that still would have been there even if she had spoken up sooner. What Dr. Noyes meant was, this wasn't Lily's fault.

But Dr. Noyes also told them the prognosis was good. She said almost everyone with this kind of cancer survives it. Dr. Noyes and all the specialists expected Anders to get better too. He started treatment and they said it was helping.

The only person who mentioned that Anders might die was Deandra, who whispered it almost excitedly, said she'd heard someone at the grocery store say it, and had Lily thought about what it would be like? That was at Lily and Anders' eleventh birthday party in March, which Anders was feeling well enough to have, and Lily was so shocked and stunned at the words coming out of Deandra's mouth that she didn't do anything to stop her. She didn't tell her off or shove her nose into the cake like she later imagined doing. She just froze, and Deandra kept talking, and Lily finally got up and walked away.

She hadn't spoken to Deandra since. At Anders' funeral thirteen days later, after an infection had swept in and killed him before any of the doctors could stop it, Lily didn't even look in her ex-friend's direction. She ignored her and ignored her and it didn't fix a thing.

11

Water's Edge

It was humid and hazy the last day of June, but the chickens didn't seem to notice. Inside, Ms. Turner was blasting a giant fan, which blew Lily's hair straight back and every which way when she accepted the invitation to "come sit for a spell" and drink a glass of iced tea.

The tea was pink and tasted both sweet and tart. "Rose hips," Ms. Turner said. "Picked them myself. You know those big bushes down near the shore at Goose Cove?"

Lily nodded, though she hadn't realized the dense, prickly bushes—which grew even taller than she was, and as wide as they were tall—were roses. Pink flowers with soft, splayed petals and fuzzy yellow centers bloomed on them in early summer. By fall, clumps of shiny, orangey-red fruit dangled from their stems. The fruit—rose hips—looked like large berries or tiny apples but with alien tentacles out the bottom, like a round, fruity version of squid.

"Bet you didn't know you could eat them," Ms. Turner said. She was right. Lily hadn't. "They make nice jam too."

Lily held her glass with both hands so it wouldn't slip— the outside was slick with condensation—and offered a fact of her own. "Did you know chickens are related to dinosaurs?"

Ms. Turner looked surprised. "Is that right?"

Lily nodded. "Not all dinosaurs. But some that laid eggs and had feathers were ancestors to birds. Actually, by some definitions, birds *are* dinosaurs." She and Anders had read up on it yesterday, in a book with really great pictures.

"Well, no wonder Frankie considers herself so tough," Ms. Turner said. Lily laughed. The orange-and-white tabby curled up on a nearby armchair flattened his ears, like they were disrupting his nap. His name was Prince, and he definitely acted like he was king of everything. Ms. Turner said he'd been that way since he was a tiny kitten.

When teatime was over, Lily washed both their glasses, said goodbye to the chickens, and started toward home. She made it only as far as the end of the dirt road before Quinn pulled up alongside her. "Hey, Safety Patrol," Quinn said.

She gave a two-finger salute off the edge of her helmet.

Lily flushed with pleasure at being given a nickname. "Hey," she replied.

"What's that?" Quinn lifted her chin toward the jar in Lily's hands.

She held it up so Quinn could see. "Rose hip jam for my mom from Ms. Turner. She makes it herself."

"Oh, I know." Quinn slid off the saddle but still straddled the bike. "She and Aunt Linda go cuckoo for canning. Every August they make a huge batch of dilly beans using Aunt Linda's green beans and Ms. Turner's dill. By the end they're, like, totally pickled off the vinegar fumes and hours of gossip and singing along to classic rock. It's a sight."

Lily grinned. That sounded fun.

"So you already fed the chickens, then?" Quinn asked. Lily nodded. "Cool. I'm gonna go dangle my feet in the ocean for a bit. It's too hot out here. You want to come?"

Lily did want that, desperately, but she couldn't. She glanced away to hide her embarrassment. "I'm not allowed to go down to the water by myself," she admitted.

Quinn's two-note laugh sounded closer to a hiccup. "What am I, your imaginary friend?"

Lily's embarrassment faded in the thrill of that word, *friend*. "Oh," she said. "I guess you're right." She was so used to *alone* meaning *without Anders*, she had forgotten she could pair off with other people. Not for everything. But at least for this. "Yeah, let's go."

Quinn led the way across the street, down the hill, and behind someone's house, to a path that curved through the woods toward the water. She left her bike and helmet in the seagrass, kicked off her shoes, and plopped herself down on a large, flat rock, facing the ocean. Lily watched her back for a few seconds, awaiting instructions that never came, then put down the jam jar, pulled off her sneakers and socks, and joined Quinn on the rock. The granite felt bumpy beneath her bare feet, but not too sharp. She was glad there were only a few barnacles.

It was high tide, or close to it, and the water came right up to the edge of where Quinn was sitting. Lily chose her own spot a little higher up, not wanting her shorts to get wet. She poked her toes into the ocean. It was cold, as expected, but the bite didn't last, so she stretched her legs down the slope of rock until the water covered her ankles. Her whole body felt instantly cooler.

"Good, right?" Quinn said. Lily agreed. It was perfect.

She eyed a mass of brown seaweed that swayed near Quinn's feet, and reminded herself it probably wasn't hiding any sea monsters. Only crabs. It was the kind of seaweed she and Anders liked to pop—the ends had swollen little balloons you could squish between your thumb and forefinger—but she didn't feel like popping it in front of Quinn. Playing with seaweed might seem immature.

The ocean was calm in this inlet—filled with ripples instead of waves. Up close, the water was silty, but farther up it seemed green and blue, reflecting sky and pine trees and sparkling in the sun. A slight breeze traveled toward them, carrying whispers from other islands that dotted Penobscot Bay, most as small as or smaller than the overlap. Lily breathed in deep to fill her nose with ocean air. Beside her, Quinn did the same.

"We're lucky it's high tide," Lily said. In a few hours, when the tide emptied out, this cove would be a long stretch of clam flats: no water, just muck, and whatever seaweed and shells got left behind. It would be impossible to dip their toes in then.

"Want to know a secret?" Quinn asked.

Lily tried not to sound too eager. "Sure."

Quinn flicked a stray hair from her eyes. "I kind of love the smell of clam flats," she said.

"You *what*?" Lily shrieked. Every kid she knew agreed the clam flats stank. Whenever they drove over the causeway toward the bridge at low tide, Anders rushed to roll the windows up before too much stink got inside. She and Deandra pretended the fumes were poison and dramatically held their breath until the putrid danger passed. Clam flats smelled like seagull poop on rotten mussels, plus seaweed, mud, and brine. She'd never heard a single person claim to like it.

In her surprise, she'd forgotten to play it cool, but Quinn seemed delighted by the overreaction. "I know they stink, but it's like . . . kind of a good stink, you know?"

Lily wrinkled her nose and shook her head vehemently. It made her vision blur, but she still caught Quinn's smile. "Yuck," she said. "Do you love stinky feet too? And dirty gym clothes? And being trapped on the school bus with eighth grader farts?"

Quinn waved her hand in front of her nose. Lily took it as encouragement to keep going. "Tomorrow I'll pack us blue cheese and bait sandwiches and we can go have a picnic at the dump," she teased.

Quinn cackled and gave her a light shove. "Very funny," she said. "I know it's weird. But I love how that smell is part of this place. When I smell it, it smells like home."

Suddenly, Lily wanted to love the scent too. Maybe next time she smelled it, she would. "We should make 'I heart clam flats' T-shirts for the tourists," she joked.

"And scratch-and-sniff postcards," Quinn said. "They'll sell way better than lobster traps and boats or lupines. Who needs to see the bridge when you can smell what rots beneath it?"

"Let's do it. We'll earn millions. You can buy your own car. You can buy ten of them!"

Quinn kicked a splash of water in Lily's direction. It sprinkled the rock and rolled down her shins. It felt nice.

Refreshing. "I do like lupines though," Lily said.

"Me too. Did you ever read that picture book? About the lady who spreads lupine seeds?"

"Yes! *Miss Rumphius.*" Lily's brain tingled at the connection. "Ms. Foster read it to us in first grade."

Quinn kicked her feet again, but not at Lily this time. "I had Ms. Foster for first grade too."

"Did you like her?" She had been one of Lily's favorite teachers.

"Yeah, but I'm still mad about the time I had to stay inside from recess just because Scott Nevells asked me how to spell *poop* and *pee*, so I told him, and Maddie Eaton tattled on us, and we both got in trouble for saying bad words. I didn't even say them! I just *spelled* them."

Lily giggled. "Did you spell them correctly?" she asked.

"Yes!" Quinn gestured wildly and salt water sprayed everywhere. "Like, what, did she not want him to *learn* in school? Was I supposed to just *not* tell him and let him remain ignorant forever?"

Lily loved that Quinn held grudges too. "It sounds like Maddie Eaton's the one to be mad at," she said.

Quinn's lips twisted and her left dimple showed. "Yeah, well. It's hard to be mad at Mads." Something about the way she said it made Lily slightly jealous of Maddie, a girl she barely knew a thing about—except that she was Quinn's real friend and Quinn's own age and impossible for Quinn to stay mad at. Envy fluttered like a moth in her chest.

"She's much less of a priss now," Quinn added, and Lily felt a little bit better.

"You definitely did the right thing," she said. "It's important to be able to spell *poop*."

"Thank you, Lily," Quinn said with a solemn expression. "Thank you for affirming my truth."

Lily kept her face equally serious. "P-E-E," she said slowly. Quinn splashed her. This time, Lily splashed back.

12

Things Go Boom

Lily was curled up on the couch, reading a book, when the explosions started. They were distant but loud enough to pull Mom out of her distractions and into Lily's orbit. "What was that?" she asked, glancing toward the ceiling like it might provide the answer.

The sky crackled and boomed, and Lily looked up from her book. "Fireworks," she said. "It's the Fourth of July."

Mom looked stricken. "Oh."

It had been a good day. Sunny and hot. Lily had gone up to Ms. Turner's first thing to see the chickens, and found a note tucked inside the feed bin, waiting on top of the bag. *Happy Indie HEN DANCE Day!* was written across the page in black pen. Beneath that was a funny—and surprisingly good—drawing of two chickens dancing. It wasn't signed, except for a *Bawk bawk* in the corner, but Lily knew the note was from Quinn. She'd tucked it carefully into her back pocket to pin to her bulletin board later.

Anders didn't show up right away in the overlap, and Lily hadn't felt like keeping still, so she'd run into the field to do some exploring. She let her fingers skim the tops of the tall grasses, which tickled her legs, and kneeled to search for wild strawberries hidden beneath their own leaves—leaves with edges that zigzagged like they'd been cut by Mom's pinking shears. (She found only one small berry, the size of her pinkie nail, and so old and mushy, she left it for the snails. Strawberries peaked in mid-June. Lily didn't hold it against them.) She watched a whirling, twirling butterfly ballet and quizzed herself on the names of wildflowers Anders had taught her.

Daisies and buttercups were the easy ones, and most prevalent, but there were also clovers, mint, thistles, and goldenrod (which sounded like a goddess's weapon but looked like a raccoon's feather duster). She saw bright yellow black-eyed Susans (flowers as hardy and tough as their name—if Lily ever took up roller derby, she'd borrow it), Queen Anne's lace (best admired from a distance, since bees and bugs loved it too), and a few pretty clumps of lavender asters (more would bloom later in summer). Along the thicket between the field and the Olsons' yard (which smelled like hamburgers and charcoal—the Olsons were having a cookout), she found a crop of touch-me-nots and jumped each time one of their soft green pods detonated against her fingertips.

She couldn't remember the real names of what she thought of as mini-daisies (*fleabane*, Anders told her later, which made her itch, so she resolved to forget it again) or the yellow and orange flowers that looked like extra tall, extra small, kind of matted dandelions (Anders couldn't remember it either, surprisingly, so Lily decreed them "mangy lions" and placed a few inside the squirrel fort). The wildflower with the best name was the tufted vetch, which had shaggy purple florets, spiky leaves, and witchy, reaching tendrils. She picked some for the vase in the kitchen.

Lily had never been as interested in what plants were called as she was in the plants themselves (same with birds, mushrooms, trees, insects, songs, state capitals, and baseball players), but she also hadn't needed to learn those things because Anders memorized all of them. Bringing him on an adventure was like bringing along a pocket field guide. His brain wasn't her own, but she'd stored half of what she knew there. She had to remember twice as much now, for both of them.

"We missed the parade," Mom said, sounding like a little kid who'd just realized she was lost. "And the fish fry. And the fun run." Three more fireworks kaboomed in quick succession. One of the neighbors' dogs barked.

"I know," Lily said.

Mom blinked. "You want to hop in the car and see if we can catch the end of the fireworks? There might be music on the pier after. Remember last year, the steel drums?"

She remembered. She, Anders, and Mom—and a whole bunch of summer people, tourists, and locals—had danced beneath the stars, surrounded by music and ocean. On one of the last songs, Mom grabbed their hands and spun them, and they'd ended the night dizzy and laughing.

Lily shook her head. Maybe it would have been fun to go downtown earlier, but she didn't want to rush to see the end of what she'd missed. "I'm almost ready for bed. I just want to finish this chapter," she said.

Mom sat on the arm of the couch and smoothed Lily's hair. Lily felt like a cat under her touch. "What are you reading?"

She used a finger to mark her spot and tilted the cover so Mom could see.

"*Rules for Stealing Stars*," Mom read aloud. "That's a good title."

"It's a good book. So far." She liked that it was full of sad things, but also magical and beautiful. She liked that the narrator's life was hard to explain, just like her own. That's what she'd say if Mom asked what it was about.

Mom stood, unfolded the couch blanket, and spread it

over Lily's bare legs. Its warmth made her realize she'd been chilly. "I'm sorry," Mom said. "About what you've missed."

Fourth of July. Anders. A regular summer. Her mom. Lily didn't ask which of those things Mom meant.

She nodded, and Mom kissed her forehead. "Good night," they each said.

Mom closed the door to her sewing room and soon the machine was whirring.

13

Sink or Swim

The next morning, Lily went down to the kitchen for breakfast and was startled to see Mom there, awake, dressed, and slicing watermelon. "Good morning," Mom said. She transferred a few wedges from the cutting board to a plastic container, and used their biggest knife to chop a few more.

"Good morning," Lily echoed. She watched Mom cautiously for a minute before pouring herself a bowl of cereal and sliding onto a wooden stool across from her. If Mom noticed Lily staring, she didn't mention it. "What are you doing?" Lily asked between bites.

"Packing our lunch." She smiled at Lily's confusion. "It's a gorgeous day and about to get hot. I'm making us a picnic and we're going to the Other Lily's Pond."

Lily grinned at Anders' nickname for what everyone else called the Lily Pond. When Lily and Anders were little and signed up for their first swimming lessons there, he'd gotten all excited, thinking that if Lily had a pond, there must be an Anders' Pond someplace too. Mom gently explained it wasn't *Lily's* pond, but named after the water lilies that grew along its edges, providing hiding spots for frogs and fish, and helping cut down on algae. Anders had seemed close to tears until Lily pointed to a puddle in their driveway and said, "Look! There's Anders' Lake!" From then on, the Lily Pond was called the Other Lily's Pond and any good puddle for splashing was Anders' namesake.

"Does your swimsuit from last year still fit?" Mom asked.

Lily tilted her bowl to sip the milk dregs. "I don't know." There was no swimming in the overlap, so she hadn't needed it yet.

"Try it on. And grab that picnic blanket from the back closet, will you?" Mom added.

Lily put her bowl and spoon in the dishwasher and froze. "Oh. I have to feed the chickens."

"That's fine," Mom said. "I'll go with you. I'd love to meet them. And I need to thank Ms. Turner for the jam and those beautiful peonies. Let's stop in on the way."

"Okay!" Lily ran upstairs to her room.

Forty minutes later, with the chickens fed and Ms. Turner thanked, they left their car by the side of the road and walked through the woods, on a path that wasn't great for flip-flops. Lily always forgot to wear sneakers for this part. She hated getting dirt in her sandals, but by lifting each foot a little higher than normal—good practice for her future playing fart hand in a marching band—she managed okay.

She stealthily picked the wedgie from her butt (the swimsuit was fine but a little tight—luckily the material stretched) and followed Mom to the grassy clearing by the edge of the pond. Mom waved to someone up ahead and called out hello. Lily stopped short.

It was Deandra's mom. And Deandra. And Lily's mother was heading straight toward them.

"Mom," Lily said. "Let's put our stuff down here."

Mom glanced over her shoulder at Lily and gestured. "Did you see? Deandra's here!"

Lily didn't look. "I want to sit in the sun."

Mom shifted the cooler to her other hand. "Are you sure? You'll roast. And our food will get hot."

"I don't care." She didn't budge.

Mom tilted her head to one side, the way Barkly did in the photo on Mom's dresser. "How about half in the shade, half out?" She stepped forward without waiting for an answer, and spread their blanket a few feet from Deandra's, which was in the shade of an oak tree. Deandra's mom, Katie, got up to hug her. Mom seemed to melt into the hug.

Lily kneeled on the edge of the blanket, as far from Deandra as possible, and busied herself with arranging her things. "Hi, Lily," Katie said.

"Hi." Lily stood. "I'm going swimming." Normally she'd let the sun warm her up more first (the Other Lily's Pond was always colder than she expected, though it was never as cold as the ocean), but *normally* she wasn't avoiding the last person on earth she wanted to see. She kicked off her flip-flops, pulled off her shirt and shorts, and waded in. It wasn't too bad for the first two steps, but by the third, her skin tingled with goose bumps.

Minnows darted away from her ankles and pond muck squished beneath her toes as she moved through the shallow water, not yet deep enough to swim. She shivered a little, reminded herself she'd get used to it, and swerved to avoid the splashes of two preschoolers with buckets. They didn't seem chilly in the least.

She remembered last summer, searching for newts here with Anders and cupping her palms to hold the few they were fast enough to catch. She wondered if Sir Nameyname Newt Name and Queen Petunia of Many Spots had lived through the frozen winter and were someplace nearby, swimming or snacking or watching her. She wondered if they remembered Anders.

When the water was up past her knees, she steeled herself and plunged in.

Lily gasped at the sudden, full-body cold, but she refused to shriek or even splash too hard, just in case Deandra was watching. She kicked her strong legs, matched her breaths to her strokes, and imagined how she looked to the birds overhead—like an enormous, elegant fish, born to move this way. In the water, her body felt graceful and free, and soon she didn't notice the temperature. She wondered if this was what death was like.

Now that she thought of it, the analogy seemed perfect. Like death, the water was strange and forbidding at first. Scary to approach. As you inched in, your heart raced with uncertainty for what was ahead. No matter how well you prepared yourself for the plunge, it was impossible not to be nervous. The water gulped you in, and the shock of it took your breath away.

But after the first instant, you adjusted and soon it was easy, lovely, fine. What were you so afraid of? Your worries glided away and you moved in completely different ways. You belonged to a new world. The water held you.

Was this how Anders felt outside the overlap? If she were the dead one, she would figure out a way to describe it.

Once she'd swum out as far as she was allowed, Lily turned back toward shore and treaded water. Her mom and Deandra's mom had their heads close together, talking. She was too far away to hear their voices, but she knew Mom was talking about Anders. Her shoulders looked sad, and Katie kept nodding and touching Mom's arm. Deandra had her face in an iPad, probably playing a new video game, and Lily hoped without hope she wasn't eavesdropping on whatever Mom was saying.

Who brought electronics to go swimming? Everything Deandra did annoyed her.

It was weird that once Lily and Deandra were friends, and now Deandra didn't know the slightest thing about her. Deandra's life, too, continued on without Lily, and Lily didn't know about that either. Like, what games was she into now? Lily neither knew nor cared, though five months ago they'd have been passing the tablet back and forth between them.

No one besides Anders knew the most important thing about Lily now. But at the same time, he understood the rest of her—the Lily outside the overlap—less and less. They'd always changed and grown together. Now they were changing apart.

Lily stopped treading and let the weight of that thought pull her under. She sank and sank, opened her eyes, and saw nothing. What if she stayed here? What if she never resurfaced? She held in place, just to see.

Her heart beat faster, swelling and thumping as if to escape her chest. Her lungs burned and screamed with the need for breath. For an excruciatingly long moment, she let them. She let herself begin to drown.

With five swift kicks, she burst back to the surface and took deep, greedy gulps of air. Drowning wouldn't reunite her with Anders. She wasn't sure how she knew, but she was certain staying alive was the only way to hold on to him.

Still sputtering and gasping, Lily swam toward shore. When she reached shallow water, she stood, coughing and shaking, while the pond water streamed from her limbs. It took all the energy she had just to hold herself up. She'd never been so exhausted.

She half expected Mom to come running with a towel— to wrap her up, hold her tight, and say thank goodness you're all right. But she wasn't surprised when it didn't happen.

No one on shore had panicked or worried about Lily. They hadn't even noticed she could have drowned.

Lily was strong. She took care of herself. Everyone knew she would be okay. In fact, they counted on it.

She got out of the pond and toweled off.

She wasn't okay.

14

What If

After a sandwich and some watermelon (eaten in peace, in the shade, while Deandra and Katie went swimming), Lily felt a lot better. Still, she said no when Mom asked if she wanted to go back in together. She'd had enough water for one day. Instead, she opened her book and sank into the story.

Katie's voice pulled her out. "Lily, what's yours?"

Lily forced herself to look up from the page. It was disorienting to be immersed in a book and get yanked out of it. "My what?" she asked.

Katie and Deandra were back on their blanket, already dried off. They stared at Lily expectantly. "Your favorite season," Katie said.

"Oh. I guess baseball." She glanced at the pond and saw Mom floating on her back, gazing at the sky, as still and calm as a lily pad.

Deandra snickered. "That's not a season."

"Yes it is. It's literally called 'baseball season,'" Lily said.

"Yeah, but it goes from, like, April to September."

"October," she corrected. "And so what?"

Deandra rolled her eyes and huffed, like it was some huge bother to answer. "So that's spring, summer, and fall. Your favorite season can't be every season except winter."

Lily shrugged. "I like winter too."

She wanted to add, "Sorry, I didn't know the question had so many rules," but it wasn't worth it. Deandra was so insufferable now, it seemed impossible she used to be fun.

Mom had stopped floating and switched to swimming. She was already pretty far out—way past where Lily had gone. Lily wanted to shout for her to turn back, but she knew Mom wouldn't hear her. She leaned forward, like that would bring them closer.

"Well, anything but mud season, right?" Katie said in her cheerful, oblivious way. "Or blackfly season, yuck. Maine really has it all."

"So why do we live here? We should move to Florida," Deandra said.

Katie laughed. "I'd much rather have blackflies and mud than poisonous snakes and alligators. No thanks."

Lily tuned them out and kept watching Mom, who looked smaller and smaller in the distance. She bit down, hard, on nothing.

Mom had never swum off like this before. If she got tired or cramped and needed help, she was too far out for Lily to reach her.

What if Mom kept going and never turned back? It wasn't the ocean; she couldn't swim out forever. But the pond was too long for Lily to see to the other side. It was big enough to get lost in. Mom could climb out and disappear into the surrounding woods, and Lily wouldn't know how to find her. If Mom wanted to vanish, Lily couldn't stop her.

It was a horrible, lurching thought. There was nothing she could do. She could only wait for Mom to swim back to her.

"What was Anders' favorite season?" Katie asked. She held out a container of purple-red grapes, all sliced in half like they were for toddlers.

Adults did this sometimes: brought up Anders casually, out of nowhere, as if to give Lily a chance to talk about him or maybe to show they hadn't forgotten. She always flinched when they spoke of him in the past tense. He wasn't past tense to her.

Lily refused the grapes and wished she could refuse the question. She didn't want Anders stuck in time as a collection of old facts. Once all those pieces from his life were compiled, that would be it—no adding any more. Years ago, Lily's favorite color was peach and today it was yellow (specifically the bright, bold yellow of the forsythia bush that bloomed near the front door in April), but in the future it might be blue, violet, or scarlet. If she pinned Anders down to one favorite color, he wouldn't get a chance to change it. He'd stay stuck as he was and wouldn't continue to grow. Same with seasons.

She knew the answer to the question though. He loved wishing season, which was what he called the months when dandelion flowers turned kitten soft and became fluffy balls of seeds just begging to be blown. But she wouldn't share that detail in front of Deandra.

"He likes summer, I guess," she said. She looked out at the pond and pulsed with relief. Mom had turned around and was swimming toward them with a slow, steady crawl.

Deandra popped another grape in her mouth. "Most people do."

Mom was shouting distance away now. Lily jumped up and waded out to meet her.

15

Drowning in Moonlight

Mom showered when they got home, but Lily changed out of her swimsuit and ran to the overlap. She figured a swim was as good as bathing—maybe better—and she had a surprise for Anders.

While fetching the picnic basket from the closet that morning, she'd spied a game they hadn't played in ages—a game that was perfect for the overlap. She set it up near the tire swing while she waited.

"Croquet!" Anders said when he appeared.

She nodded proudly. "Do you remember the rules?" She'd found the equipment in the closet but no instructions.

He looked at the metal hoops pressed into the ground and shrugged. "Not really. Do you?"

"Not exactly," she admitted. "Not all of them."

"Oh, good." He picked up a mallet. "That means we can invent our own. Rule One: You can only hit a ball while standing on one foot."

"Okay," she said. "Rule Two: Every four turns, each player gets to move a wicket."

Anders grinned and took a practice stroke. "Croquet chaos. I like it. Rule Three: Dead kid starts. I'm blue, green, and orange." He kicked her butt in two rounds before forfeiting a third, but she didn't pout. Now that he was dead, she was better about losing.

That night, her hair and skin smelled faintly of pond water—a lighter and cleaner scent than that of the pond down the hill from the house, but clearly related. That pond was too shallow for swimming and was composed more of muck than water. But in winter it was perfect for skating and lying on the ice to stargaze as the afternoon turned from dusk to dark. In summer it was best for frog gazing or watching skinny-legged water striders glide across the surface while shiny blue dragonflies darted above. If she plunged her arms into that pond to pull up cattails or catch toads, bathing afterward wasn't optional.

She sank into sleep and dreamed of an underwater tea party with everything sliced in half—teapots, saucers, petits fours, sandwiches. The other guests asked question after question, but with half the words gone from each query, she had no idea how to answer. She balanced on half a seaweed chair and held out a pinkie to lift her half teacup, but the chair floated upward, and the ocean got smaller and smaller, and soon she was swimming with all her might to try to stay beneath the surface, certain if her head went above water, she'd drown. She opened her mouth to call for Anders, but the ocean was a tiny cube now, too small for him to get in or her scream to get out.

She startled awake and sat up in bed, fighting her sheets and her terror. The dream raced through her veins. She released its last wisps in an exhale.

The room was dim and her clock said 11:53, but the curtains Mom made from the yellow fabric Lily chose were so luminous, it almost seemed like daytime. She peeked behind them and saw the moon, full and bright, casting a cool blue glow and long shadows across the field. She pulled a sweater on over her pajamas; tiptoed downstairs, past the closed sewing room door with a light shining underneath; and slipped out the back door.

Outside, the moon beamed even brighter. Lily breathed it in and looked for stars, but the moon outshone most of them. She walked cautiously across the dirt-and-pebble driveway, then broke into a run. The grass was cold and damp beneath her bare feet, but she felt warmed by the adventure. It was exhilarating.

She'd never been outside by herself this close to midnight, and she'd never seen the field look quite like this. The most familiar place in the world to her was suddenly, magically different. She wished she could share it with Anders.

She turned toward the overlap and sat on the tire swing to wait. It swayed a little, then stilled, and as her eyes adjusted to the moonlight, the sounds of nighttime swirled around her. "Anders?" she said softly.

She'd never looked for him in the dark before, since he always vanished at dusk. But tonight wasn't dark. Anything seemed possible.

Besides, their whole lives, he always showed up when she needed him. "I'm here," she whispered.

The wind whispered back through the leaves and grass. A bat dipped and swooped, cutting through the air, elegant and swift. A lone bullfrog croaked in the pond and crickets answered. Anders didn't appear.

She shivered and pulled her sleeves over her hands.

In daytime, when she entered the overlap without him, it still felt like their space. After midnight, it felt like the moon's.

Her skin prickled with dawning awareness of someone or something behind her.

She turned very slowly and gasped. The half-finished breath stuck to her throat, and it took several seconds to understand what she was seeing and release it.

Less than ten feet away, standing rigid as a statue, a deer stared back through the non-dark. Lily breathed as slowly as she could, though her pulse still galloped, and did not blink or move as she watched it. Intense energy stretched between them like a taut rubber band.

The deer startled, the tension snapped, and not one but three deer ran away from her. They leaped through the field, both majestic in their soaring and silly in their fright. Their pert white tails disappeared from sight long before they reached the edge of the woods, as though they vanished into another world or dimension.

Lily squinted into the distance and wondered if this was what Anders saw when he tried to look past the borders of the overlap. Despite the brightness of the moon, it was like opening her eyes underwater—everything appeared slightly blurred and not quite to be trusted. Only when she shifted her gaze back to things that were close was she able to focus.

The night seemed enormous. Lily felt neither large nor small in it, only present.

"You're missing it," she whispered to Anders. She stared at the moon and imagined it knew how much she was missing him.

16

Deep in the Night

At the far end of the field, where tall grasses met birch, and scents changed from sun-grown to shade-soaked, three deer slowed their steps. One looked back.

His companions waited.

The buck stretched his neck in the direction of the girl and bleated softly, as though comforting a worried fawn.

From a nearby tree, a great horned owl added its call.

The deer listened to the calm of the still, clear night, flicked their tails, bowed their heads, and ran on.

17

Cranky Pants

The next day, Mom stayed in her room, Quinn flew past extra early on her bike, the breakfast milk was sour, the chickens seemed to be squabbling, and Anders didn't show up for ages. When he finally appeared, Lily was cranky. "Do you want me to go?" he asked after the third time she snapped at him. "We don't have to hang out if you'd rather be someplace else."

"No!" she practically shouted. She stomped her foot and crossed her arms. She felt ridiculous and horrible, but she couldn't stop. "That's not what I want at all."

"Ohhhhhkay," Anders said.

She sank to the ground. "I'm tired."

"From staying up all night with the moon," he said,

nodding sagely, and she wanted to smack him.

"No, from sitting around all day waiting for you to finally get here so we can play."

His eyebrows went up. "Hey, I know what we should do. Let's play 'taking a nap.' Doesn't that sound fun?"

She threw her book at him and missed. It flew past his shoulder and landed all splayed out, with the cover open and the pages bent, and she felt instant regret.

"Sorry. I'm sorry," she said, apologizing to the book as well. "You're right. I'm just . . . I do need a nap."

His lips twitched.

"I didn't eat enough lunch. I'm hungry and I'm exhausted, and that's why you seem so incredibly annoying," she said.

"And why your aim is so bad," he added.

She rolled her eyes and held out her hand. "Just give me the book."

Anders hesitated. Lily groaned. "I said I'm sorry! What do you want me to do, beg?"

He didn't move, just looked at her sadly.

"Give me the book! I don't want to get up. Please?" She felt irrationally desperate and increasingly unwilling to move. She just wanted him to hand it to her so they could move on. "C'mon, it's right behind you."

"I can't." He hung his head and his shoulders drooped. If he was teasing to cheer her up, it wasn't working.

"Anders! You're not funny."

He flinched. "I'm not trying to be. It's that I can't—"

"Fine!" Lily cut him off. "I'll get it myself." She pushed up and stormed past him.

"Lily," he said, his tone careful, as she brushed off the book and put it in her backpack. She ignored him. "Hey. I'm trying to tell you something."

"What," she growled in a voice that screamed *I don't want to hear it.*

He looked away. "Never mind."

But it was too late. Despite how desperately she tried not to, deep down, she already knew. She felt it in the pit of her stomach.

The dandelion he couldn't see. The book he wouldn't get. The croquet game he quit when a ball went astray. The paper airplane he wouldn't reach for when it landed just inside the boundary.

She closed her eyes, but the truth came flooding in cold and fast like the ocean.

18

The Terrible Truth

S he knew.

She knew, she knew, and she didn't want to know. She'd ignored every awful sign of it for weeks.

But that didn't change it.

"The overlap," she whispered.

Anders nodded, and she lost all hope he might be talking about something else—something that wouldn't destroy her.

He met her eyes and said it. "It's shrinking."

19

Unbearable, Unacceptable, and Utterly Unfair

Lily wanted to scream.

She wanted to kick things and argue and fight this. She'd stage a protest. She'd go on strike. She would start a petition to stop it.

She would not take it lying down.

But there was no one to shout at, no place to appeal. She could glare at the boundaries and yell at the sky, but they wouldn't be moved by her pleas and frustration. They did not care what was fair. She couldn't bargain, trade, threaten, beg, or negotiate her way out of this. She didn't have a single solution.

All she had was Anders, and the thought of losing him again made her shatter into a billion tiny pieces.

But she couldn't afford to break.

Anders looked at her with an old, familiar expression—one that asked, *What should we do?* One that trusted she would have an answer.

Lily didn't have an answer.

So she would find one. *They* would find one. She wouldn't let him down.

She got out her notebook and favorite green pen. "Okay," she said. "We need a plan."

20

Easier Said Than Done

Lily stared at the blank page. The page stared back, blankly. She tapped her pen against it and thought.

She had no idea what to write, but she needed to write *something* because Anders was watching and waiting. He was counting on her to come up with a plan.

"Okay," she said again, in the most authoritative voice she could muster. It worked. She felt a little more confident just hearing it.

"First things first," she added. That sounded good too.

She wrote a green *1* at the top of the page, and put a small dot right after, which looked nice and official. She considered adding a second dot but decided that might ruin the effect.

Anders leaned closer to peek at the page, and she panicked. She had no first step. If the overlap was shrinking, what could they possibly do? Nothing.

She shoved that thought away. Her brother was counting on her. She would not fail him again. She put pen to page and, without knowing what she would write, scrawled *Collect facts.*

There.

She looked at her twin. His forehead wrinkled.

"Collect facts?" he read, as if it were a question, not a plan.

"Yes," Lily said. "And . . ." She lifted the pen and added, *2. Define the questions.*

Anders stared at the page, then at her.

She swallowed. "Those two steps should probably actually be reversed," she said, and drew a little arrow in the margin to switch them.

Anders didn't look any less confused, but Lily felt increasingly certain. "It's like what Ms. Thompson said in science class," she explained. "Before we can find our answers, we need to know exactly what the questions are. Then we can go on our fact-finding mission."

Anders nodded slowly, and she felt a surge of hope. Maybe she did have a plan. Maybe the plan would work.

"So. We know the overlap is shrinking, but how fast and by how much? Also *why*?" she said. Her chest squeezed at that last one. She kept going. "We need to collect as much information as possible, so we'll know exactly what we're dealing with. The better we understand what's happening, the better chance we have of finding a way to stop it. Or reverse it."

Putting it that way got her excited. If they could figure out how the overlap worked, maybe they could expand it. Then they could be in the whole world together, at least when no one else was around.

It was okay that Anders seemed skeptical. He often wasn't sold on Lily's best ideas at first. But at least now they had a plan.

A plan she hoped would save them both.

21

The Plan in Action

For weeks, it was all Lily could think about.

She carried the notebook wherever she went, and slept with it under her pillow in case anything noteworthy occurred to her in her sleep.

In the mornings she awoke early, scarfed down breakfast, and ran instead of walked up the hill to Ms. Turner's. She fed the chickens without sitting to pet them, and gave Ms. Turner only a quick wave. When she ran into Quinn, they didn't talk long. She had to return to the overlap.

She wore a watch and recorded what time Anders appeared or vanished, so she could calculate how many minutes they were together each day.

She noted the weather, the wind, and the position of the

sun, in case any of that proved to be relevant.

She borrowed a measuring tape, several spools of white thread, and a box of pins from Mom's sewing stuff. ("Hmm? Sure, of course," Mom said when Lily asked permission. She'd prepared a careful excuse as to why she needed them, but Mom was lost in a sad day and didn't ask.) Every day, sometimes twice a day, Anders slowly walked the perimeter of where he could go, while Lily unspooled the thread and pinned it to the ground to mark the new edges. This task took so long, she often stayed out alone with a flashlight after dusk to measure how far things had shifted.

All the numbers went down in the notebook, alongside her growing list of questions.

It was reassuring to learn that although the overlap shrank steadily, it contracted by only an inch or two per day. Those inches added up faster than Lily would have liked, but they still had a lot of space left, which meant they had time to figure things out. Whenever she worried the overlap might simply disappear, she reviewed the data and assured herself it would all add up to answers. They just had to keep collecting it.

Anders wasn't so sure. He definitely wasn't as eager.

The more determined Lily got, the more he sighed and dragged his feet. The more she talked about numbers and facts, the less attention he paid to what she was saying. The daily testing, unspooling, pinning, and measuring made Lily feel like at least she was *doing* something. It made Anders fidget.

"Want to hunt for four-leaf clovers?" he asked on an overcast day in late July, when they'd been measuring and observing for three weeks and one day. She didn't answer or look up from the string she was pinning next to his little toe. He shuffled in a silly dance move, knocking the spool over with his foot. She jumped.

"Don't move!" she said. "Stay on the border. If you move, I might mark it wrong."

"Bet I can find one faster than you," he said, trying to bait her.

Lily loved winning. She never turned down a contest or dare. But she ignored him. This wasn't a game. She would not let him distract her.

"Clover dover schmover brover," he chanted, keeping his feet in place while shaking his behind.

Lily shot him a warning glance. He broke into song. "Row, row, row your butt! Gently down the stream. Merrily, merrily, merrily, merrily, like your butt's a dream."

"Anders!" she snapped.

The dance stopped. "You never want to do anything fun anymore," Anders said.

Lily sat up straight. "Ignoring the problem won't make

it go away," she pointed out.

He crossed his arms. "Neither will thinking about it every single second."

They stared at each other for a very long moment. Just before Anders softened, Lily blew out her breath like a bull. "Fine," she said sharply.

"Fine," he said, less so.

She pointed. "We'll measure to there, then break for clover." It wouldn't hurt for them to find a little luck.

Anders smiled. "And croquet?"

Her heart twisted. "No." Anders always dealt with things that scared him by pretending they didn't exist—like adults said to do with bullies. *Just ignore them and they'll go away!* Like he'd tried to do with his cancer.

Lily dealt with her fears by taking charge and fixing things—like she should have done when he first got sick.

This time, she wouldn't delay.

This time, she wouldn't fail him.

She couldn't measure the overlap without him, but she could take in all the facts, study, and solve them. Once she'd figured out how to stop this, they could goof around and dilly-dally to his heart's content. Until then, she had a job to do.

She had to find a way to control it. She just had to.

22

A Different Shock

The next morning, Lily woke up to rain. She peered behind the curtain at the steadily falling raindrops, frowned, and climbed back into bed.

Anders never showed up in the rain, not even when it was just misting.

She pulled the notebook out from under her pillow, clicked the top of her pen, and reviewed the numbers and facts, hoping a solution might pop out at her.

Nothing.

But she'd only been working on the problem for twenty-three days. Already she had so much more information. Surely she was almost there.

She closed the notebook, slid out of bed, and pulled on

a T-shirt and leggings. Ms. Turner's boot had come off three days ago—her ankle was finally healed—so Lily didn't have to go feed the chickens. Ms. Turner had told her to come back anytime, said that she and the girls would be glad to see her. And Lily missed them, especially Frankie. But the chickens didn't need her now. Anders did.

Her stomach grumbled.

When she stepped out of her room, she heard an odd sound, sort of like the honks of the wild geese that sometimes landed in the field. (Why didn't they choose the pond, like the great blue herons did? Geese were such funny creatures. They clearly considered themselves elegant and important, but their waddles and sudden squawking frenzies always made Lily laugh.) The honk sounded again, and Lily realized it was close—coming from the bathroom—and it wasn't so much silly as sad.

She walked closer to the door and heard running water. Mom was in there, taking a shower. Taking a shower and crying.

Lily knocked lightly on the door and pressed her ear against it. "Mom?" she said. The water kept running but the sobbing stopped.

After a long pause, Mom said, "Yeah?" in an almost-normal voice, though Lily heard it hitch.

She tried the doorknob. It was locked.

"I'm in the shower, Lily. I'll be out in a minute. Do you

need something?" Mom said. She didn't sound like sobbing Mom. She sounded like I-need-space-please-leave-me-alone-for-a-bit Mom.

Yes, Lily thought. She did need something. But she didn't know how to explain it, and she wasn't sure Mom could provide it. Mom had her own problems to deal with. "No. Never mind," she said, and went downstairs for break-fast.

There was no milk for cereal, but someone had brought them a round loaf of bread, so she fixed herself some toast with Ms. Turner's homemade jam. When her plate was empty, she sat at the kitchen counter, staring out the window and willing the rain to stop. Maybe she would go outside any-way. She'd get wet, of course, but it was plenty warm and she could wear her purple raincoat. Maybe Anders had never shown up in the rain because she hadn't waited for him long enough. She could sit out there all day, until her fingers wrinkled and her clothes were soaked, and find out. She would have to leave the notebook inside, but the mea-suring tape would do fine being damp. She'd just have to memorize the numbers.

She slid off the stool, eager to get going. But as she reached for her dirty dishes, she heard a rumble of thunder and the excitement whooshed out of her. She knew better than to go outside in a thunderstorm. If Anders saw her, he'd never let her hear the end of it.

She trudged to the bottom of the stairs and heard the shower still running. A bolt of fear chased her up the steps. She knocked on the bathroom door again. "Mom?"

"Yes?" Mom answered more quickly this time, which Lily took as a good sign. She'd been in the shower forever, which wasn't great, but it was an improvement for her to be up in the morning and bathing.

"I heard thunder," Lily said through the door, and Mom shut off the water immediately.

Mom never used to take long showers—sometimes, when the well was low, she even turned the water off while she soaped up—though as far as Lily knew, she didn't use to cry in there either. For a while after Anders died, Mom often didn't shower at all, and Lily was glad she now had the energy. But she wished Mom would pay attention to dangers like thunder. Lily couldn't afford to lose her too, and she couldn't watch both Mom and the overlap.

"Thank you. I'm getting out," Mom called.

Lily relaxed at the clink of the shower curtain rings and returned to her room.

It was Anders who'd told them the story he heard about a classmate's uncle who was washing dishes and got jolted by lightning that traveled through the kitchen pipes. Mom insisted it couldn't be true, that not using water during a thunderstorm was surely based on misconception, like the idea that having wet hair outside would give you a cold, or the fear that swallowing a watermelon seed would make a watermelon grow in your belly. But they'd looked it up and found out it was true—you really could be struck by lightning that way.

The classmate's uncle hadn't died—just experienced a real shock and lived to tell a good tale—but Anders made Mom and Lily promise never to turn on a faucet in a thunderstorm. Lily kept the promise but never spent any time worrying about it—she knew Anders had the worrying covered. But since Anders wasn't here, Lily had to be the worrywart now.

Come to think of it, Anders didn't seem to worry about much of anything these days, whereas Lily worried pretty much constantly. It was like they had switched positions. That seemed like an important change.

She opened the notebook and started a new page of questions. *Has Anders stopped worrying?* she wrote. And, *Should I be worried about that?*

She tapped her pen against the paper and wondered how to measure those kinds of answers.

23

The Outside World

One strange thing about being trapped inside all day with Anders gone and Mom awake but absorbed in her own world was the realization of how enormous their house was. It had always seemed cozy and perfect for the three of them. For two, it seemed cavernous and gloomy. The million raindrops splatting against the windows didn't help her feel any less lonely.

She stared outside through the blurry panes, half wondering if Quinn might bike past. It was both a letdown and a relief that she didn't. This weather wasn't safe for biking either.

Lily turned on the lights in her room and the hallway, even though it was daytime. She considered turning a light on in Anders' room too, but worried that might freak Mom out if she saw it. She made herself a nest of blankets on the bed and chose an old book for company. She didn't get lost in the story though. She was mostly just turning pages.

Still, it surprised her when Mom's footsteps creaked on the steps and Mom stuck her head into Lily's bedroom. "I'm going to Burnt Cove. Want to come?" she asked, and Lily jumped up quickly, before Mom could remember to be too depressed for grocery shopping.

Lily slid open the big barn doors, careful of the one with a loose roller that sometimes came off the track, and buckled up inside the Subaru. Mom backed the car out of the barn and raindrops drummed on the rooftop. The windshield wipers whooshed back and forth, pushing around streams of water. They squeaked and thunked as they danced. Lily worried suddenly whether it was safe to drive in rain coming down this hard, but Mom looked relaxed as she pulled out onto the road and switched on Maine Public Radio. Familiar voices filled the car, but Lily didn't listen to what they were saying.

She watched Mom out of the corner of her eye and tried to evaluate how she was doing. She looked much better than she had the first few weeks after Anders died. Her eyelids were less puffy and the dark smudges below them had faded a bit. She'd showered, eaten, gotten dressed in real clothes, and left the house to run errands—those all seemed like good signs. She kept closer-to-normal hours now. She sometimes spoke with people other than the psychic.

But her face was deeply weary in a way it never used to be. She smiled less often, and her smile rarely reached her eyes. Her cheeks and jawline seemed sharper, bonier, and she'd gotten so thin, it looked like it would hurt to hug her.

Lily knew from experience that Mom's hugs did hurt, but not because of pokes or jabs—because of emptiness. Because of missing. Being wrapped in Mom's sadness made it harder to escape her own. And the hugs always ended, but Lily wanted one that was permanent. One that could fix things forever and make them both happy.

Maybe once she figured out how to stabilize the overlap, they should find a way to invite Mom into it.

Maybe even before that, she should tell Mom the overlap existed—that she had seen Anders, seen him a lot, actually, and he was okay. That the afterlife wasn't like what Lorelei said, and Anders couldn't really explain most of it, but in the overlap, he was still himself, and still hers. If she told Mom all that, maybe Mom could be less sad, like Lily.

But if Mom didn't believe her, it would make everything worse. It would make Mom worry about Lily, which Lily had been working hard to avoid. Mom might start monitoring her more closely or even forbid her from spending all her time out there.

She couldn't afford those risks. And she couldn't prove

he truly existed. The overlap was an Us Thing, and if anyone else was watching, Anders might never appear.

Lily was the one he came back for. And some tiny, selfish part of her liked keeping him all to herself.

There were a lot of empty spaces in the parking lot at Burnt Cove Market, so Lily had to dash only a few yards to the door, but when she got inside, her face was streaked with rain and Mom's shirt was covered in splotches. An older man wearing a faded camouflage cap and loose jeans nodded in their direction as Lily grabbed a cart. "How you doin', dear?" he said, pronouncing *dear* as if it were two syllables and spelled with an *h* at the end: *dee-uh*.

Lily thought of the funny sign someone put up during the pandemic: *Wear a mask, Wash your hands, Stay wicked fah apaht*. She didn't have a real down east accent, but she loved the way some islanders, especially old-timers, talked, dropping the *r* from the end of some words and adding one onto others. Whenever she and Deandra went "up to camp" with Deandra's grandparents (as they called spending the weekend at Dreamwood, their summer cabin "out in the willy-wacks," with no running water or electricity, way down at the end of a long dirt road), she always came home with fun new expressions to tell Anders. Like Elwood saying Deandra "went through here like a fart in a mitten," or Wilda commenting of a neighbor, "She'd hold strong in a stiff breeze" (to which Elwood replied, "Ain't that the truth"). They both exclaimed "great gobs of goose grease" instead of "oh my gosh," and told Lily "keep it in your sneaker" when something was top secret.

She loved hearing Elwood call people "dear," "cap," or "cappy dog" and tell tales about when it was so cold, his shadow froze to the pavement. She hadn't liked it, though, when Deandra had called her "from away" and, when Lily protested that she and Anders were born here, Elwood winked and said, "Just 'cause a cat had kittens in an oven don't make 'em biscuits." That remark was, as Wilda would say, "an awful acting thing."

Mom placed a hand on the shopping cart. "We're all right," she told the man who'd asked.

He hitched his pants, said "glad to hear it" (*tuh heuhyit*, Lily pictured she'd spell that), and strolled out toward his truck like he didn't give a whit about the rain. Mom stared after him absently and Lily glanced toward the checkout line. Anders' friend Kenny was there with his dad, unloading groceries at one of the two registers and goofing around with his sister, Marlaina. Lily quickly looked away and hoped he wouldn't see her. She didn't want to say hi.

"Oh," Mom said, patting her jeans pockets. "Oh no." Her face wilted. "I forgot the list." She gaped at Lily like something awful had happened and she wasn't sure how they'd recover.

"It's okay," Lily said, before Mom could fall apart. She steered their cart around a tourist at the postcard spinner, and into the heart of the store. Mom followed. "I know what to get," she fudged, because Mom needed her to.

Aisle by aisle, she would figure it out.

24

An Unexpected Invitation

On the second day of thunder and lightning, Lily sat at the kitchen counter and moped. She pushed the soggy bits of cereal around in her leftover milk, and hit the sides of the bowl with her spoon in a way she knew would annoy Anders if only he were around to hear it. *Clink, clink, clink* went the spoon for the forty-sixth time when, outside, she heard a crunch, and an unfamiliar car pulled into the driveway. Someone jumped out the driver's side and ran up the path, holding a sweatshirt over their head for cover. A second later, there was a knock at the back door. Lily opened it, and there stood Quinn.

"Hi," Lily said.

"Hey," Quinn replied, slightly breathless. Water poured

down behind her, so Lily stepped back to let her inside. Quinn stood on the doormat and glanced around, but her eyes returned quickly to Lily. "Get your stuff. I'm kidnapping you. I need someone to play board games and drink hot chocolate with," she said.

Lily stared at her in surprise. "Where are your normal friends?" she asked before she could think better of it.

Quinn ticked the answer off on her fingers. "Sara's at camp, Mads and her dad went to Bangor to run errands and see a movie, Nolan and I hung out yesterday, Avery's working as a dishwasher at Haystack, and Payton's essentially grounded all summer. Not that I'd call any of them *normal*," she added. "We wouldn't be friends if they were."

"And you're . . . you'll be driving us?" Lily said. She wasn't stalling on purpose. It just was taking her brain a minute to catch up to this turn of events. And she didn't think it was wise to drive with someone who didn't yet have a license.

"My mother's in the car. She's probably moved over to the driver's seat by now. Don't worry; we'll keep you safe. This isn't that kind of kidnapping." Quinn lifted both eyebrows. "Any more questions?"

"I have to come home if it stops raining," Lily said, thinking out loud. Quinn nodded like that seemed reasonable. "And I need to tell my mom where I'm going."

"Of course."

Lily ran upstairs to get her backpack, which would keep the notebook dry.

Climbing into the back seat of the light blue hatchback in the driveway, Lily said hello to Quinn's mom, who introduced herself as Ellen, and slid over to make room for Quinn. Quinn didn't follow her into the back though, the way a friend her own age might have done. Instead, she buckled into the front passenger seat and cranked up the song on the stereo. Ellen caught Lily's eye in the rearview mirror and winked before turning the car around and steering them on their way.

It was a brief ride to Quinn's house—just long enough for the pop song to end—but by the time they got there, Lily's anticipation and curiosity were so big, she thought she might burst. Being allowed inside Quinn's home—inside her bedroom too, maybe—was like getting to watch a deep-sea camera explore parts of the ocean where no human had gone before. Not that humans hadn't been inside Quinn's house. Of course they had. But Lily hadn't. She had a million guesses and no idea what it might actually be like.

She didn't see much of the outside of the gray, one-story house—the rain made the car windows foggy and meant they all hurried inside—but as they took off their wet shoes in the small entryway and Quinn bickered with her mom about something to do with parallel parking, Lily took the opportunity to stare into the wood-paneled room ahead.

She saw a dark brown couch with colorful throw pillows and a beige, comfy-looking armchair facing an enormous, wall-mounted television, which was off. The coffee table in front of the couch was strewn with papers, books, and mugs, and the shelf below the television held about a dozen framed photos she would have to get closer to make out.

She peeked around the open doorframe and saw the room was larger than she had thought. Several feet behind the couch there was a dining area with a circular wooden table and chairs, and beyond that, a cutout in the wall revealed the kitchen. There wasn't anything particularly unusual about the house that she could see—it was much more ordinary than what she had imagined for Quinn—but it was cozy and inviting and she loved it. She loved being there.

Quinn noticed her gawking and smirked. "Want a tour, Safety Patrol?" she asked.

Lily's cheeks reddened. "Sure."

Quinn led her around the room, waving her arms at various objects like an old-fashioned game show host showing off prizes. "Behold, the most awkward school photo of all time," she said, pointing to a framed photo of herself a few years younger, with braces, uneven bangs, and a wide-eyed, startled expression. She swept a hand through the air above the messy coffee table. "Here we have my mother's homework, plus an exclusive collection of last year's *TV Guide*s.

Read all about what you didn't watch nine months ago! If you're in need of a few coins or old popcorn kernels, be sure to check between the couch cushions."

"Speaking of which, are you planning to vacuum today?" Ellen said from the other side of the room. Quinn dodged the question by stepping into a hallway. Lily hustled after her. She wondered if Quinn was always like this in front of her mother.

"In this room, we have the porcelain throne, the small brushes just for teeth, and a sink with hot *and* cold water taps!" Quinn announced outside the bathroom, which had green towels on three hooks, and a black-and-white geometric shower curtain. Green and blue fish swam on the wall tiles. "Behind that closed door, my parents sleep." She gripped the handle of another door across from it. "And are you ready for the main attraction?" she asked. Lily nodded. Quinn pushed open the door and said, "Ta-da!" revealing her lilac-walled bedroom. They stepped inside.

"Wow," Lily said, spinning in a slow circle to take it all in. The rest of the house may have been normal, but this room for sure felt like Quinn's. There were things to look at *everywhere*. A full-length mirror with photos of friends taped all around it, covering the frame and much of the surrounding wall too. Books and comics stacked on the floor, on a chair, and stuffed in the squat, insufficient bookshelf. Piles of bracelets and earrings next to four half-burned candles on the dresser. Clothes strewn all over the carpet, across the bunk bed, over the chair, and spilling out the half-open closet. And on the wall above the desk, dozens of colorful drawings of fantastical landscapes and creatures—intricate, beautiful drawings Lily wanted to stare at until she'd absorbed every detail.

"You made these?" she asked, and moved closer to one. A fierce, elegant dragon fought—or embraced?—a thorny and flowering goddess, who entangled its wings in her vines. In the drawing next to that, a girl wrapped in shadows stood at the edge of a cliff, extending one hand into the air beyond it. Lily felt like she was getting a glimpse inside Quinn's brain, or at least at her imagination. It was magical.

"Yeah," Quinn said. "Most of them. Payton did that one." She motioned toward a portrait of herself Lily thought was pretty good, but nowhere near as good as Quinn's drawings.

"They're incredible. You're really talented."

"Thanks," Quinn said. Lily could have looked at her artwork all day, but Quinn was already ushering her into the hallway. She reluctantly went along.

"Which bed do you sleep on?" she asked, not quite ready to leave Quinn's room behind.

"The bottom one," Quinn said. "The top bunk is my sister's when she's here."

"Oh." Lily hadn't known Quinn had a sister. "Where is

she when she isn't here?" she asked.

"Right now, Vermont. She's working on a goat farm for the summer, but usually she's at college or her mom's place in Ellsworth. She has her own room there. Technically we're half sisters. She's almost twenty-one."

"Cool," Lily said.

"Yeah," Quinn agreed.

She wanted to ask *What's her name?* and *Are you close?* and *Does she look like you?* and *Do you stay up late talking when you're sharing a room?* and *What kinds of things do you tell her?* and *Are some of those clothes all over the place hers?*, but Quinn was already walking toward the kitchen, and she didn't want to annoy her with questions. Not that Quinn ever acted annoyed with Lily. But it seemed better not to push that.

Quinn opened a red cabinet above the kitchen sink. "Do you want marshmallows or no marshmallows?"

"Marshmallows, please," Lily said.

Quinn took out two packets of cocoa mix and shook them to settle the contents. She ripped off the tops, dumped the powder and mini marshmallows into mugs, and poured the whistling kettle. Lily figured Ellen must have put the water on to boil. It was nice that it was already hot.

Quinn handed Lily the Mariner Pride mug, taking the Born to Fish one for herself, and led her to a braided rag rug in front of the woodstove, which had a real fire burning.

Lily had just managed to set her butt down on the rug without spilling her cocoa when Ellen came into the room. "Oh good, I was hoping you'd sit by the fire," she said. Her voice was as cheerful as her bright pink lipstick, which Lily didn't remember seeing in the car. "It's warm enough we don't need it, but it takes some of the edge off the gloom, doesn't it? I'm good for about half a day of rain before I get antsy and glum. The gardens and wells sure need it though, so thank goodness for that."

"Mom," Quinn said flatly.

Ellen waved. "Sorry! I'll leave you to your game. I'm right over there doing homework if you need anything, Lily, so just holler."

Quinn rolled her eyes toward the ceiling, but Lily said thank you and meant it. Quinn's mom seemed super nice.

"Does your mom really have homework?" she asked as Quinn pulled a stack of games from a cupboard.

"Yup," Quinn said. "Qwirkle, Sorry!, Scrabble, chess, checkers, Set, or Clue?"

"Qwirkle," Lily said. She'd played it at a sleepover before and liked it. She was pretty sure she remembered how.

Quinn opened the game box and removed a bag of tiles. "She dropped out of high school when she was sixteen and thought she'd be fine with a GED. But then she got really into stuff about sustainable fisheries and global warming, and ways to protect the industry and the environment, and now she's taking classes at UMO to get her degree in university studies with a minor in Maine studies. She's hoping to graduate in May. She just has a few more credits to go."

Lily heard the pride in Quinn's voice, and it made her heart swell a little. "That's awesome," she said.

Quinn nodded and held out the bag. "Take six tiles," she instructed. Lily did as she was told. "Oldest starts."

Lily blew on her cocoa and took a small sip—still too hot—as Quinn contemplated her first move. Quinn placed an orange square and an orange diamond side by side on the rug.

"Two points," Quinn said. "Oh, we need a pen and paper for keeping score." She glanced around.

Lily stood. "I've got it," she said, and went to grab the notebook from her backpack. Quinn watched her return.

"Cool notebook," Quinn said.

Lily regarded the sparkles and rainbows on the cover. They were aggressively cheerful, but nice. She liked it too. "Thanks. It was a gift from Ms. Weed."

"The guidance counselor?"

"Yeah. She gave it to me on the last day of school with this note." She flipped open the cover and showed Quinn the Post-it stuck to the back. In Ms. Weed's tall, loopy penmanship, it said: *Call anytime. I'll be thinking of you*, and gave her phone number. It felt weird and kind of special to have a teacher's personal number and permission to use it, even though Lily knew she wouldn't. Still, she'd tucked the Post-it inside the front cover to make sure it wouldn't get lost.

"Have you called her?" Quinn asked.

"What? No," Lily said. "I wouldn't do that."

"Why not? She said you should."

Lily shrugged and turned to a fresh, smooth page in the middle. "I haven't wanted to." She wrote *Quinn* on one side of the page and *Lily* on the other. Beneath Quinn's name, she made two tally marks. She looked up. Quinn was eyeing her closely.

"You know," Quinn said, so casually they could have been discussing the weather, "sometimes it helps to tell someone what you're feeling."

Lily sighed and relaxed her grip on the pen. "That's what Anders says too," she admitted.

Quinn tilted her head. Lily gulped back her mistake.

"I mean, that's what he *said*. Used to say," she corrected, and swallowed hard. It felt horrible to make him past tense.

Quinn held still and waited for her to go on. She didn't. "Well," Quinn said finally, "I think he's right. And if there's ever anything you want to spill, I'm around." She stretched her legs out on the rug. "I am very good at keeping secrets."

For one wild moment, Lily imagined showing Quinn what was in the notebook. Telling her about Anders and the overlap. Explaining the depths of her worries and calculations. Trusting Quinn with the whole truth.

But Lily couldn't do any of that. She could no more cross that line than Anders could cross out of the overlap. Instead, she said "Thanks," played her tiles, and marked her points. She reached into the bag for replacements.

Thunder rumbled outside and through her, churning the secrets she held inside. She sipped a melted marshmallow from her cup and waited for Quinn's next move.

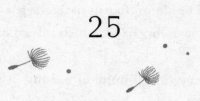

25

Pushing Back

On the third day of rain, once Lily was quite sure the danger of lightning had passed, she put on her raincoat and went outside to see if she could get Anders to appear. She figured he probably wouldn't, but it was important to test the theory. Just in case, she told herself.

Besides, she was sick of staying inside.

For the first twenty-eight minutes (she'd worn her watch, which was waterproof), it was kind of fun getting drenched out there. She checked on the boundary strings (neither raccoons nor rain had moved them); cleared the wilted mangy lions from the squirrel fort; admired the intense colors of the bark, lichen, and leaves (she'd never noticed before that trees looked more vivid in the rain); searched for but found zero four-leaf clovers; and glanced at her watch exactly three and a half times. (The almost fourth time, she got distracted by a huge new mole on her hand, which turned out to be only mud.)

By the twenty-ninth minute, waiting in the rain was getting uncomfortable. Her underwear kept bunching and her leggings were soaked through, and even the skin under her raincoat felt itchy and damp. Her hair kept sticking to her face and neck. Her sneakers sloshed with every step. The ground was soggy, the grass was slippery, and her fingers were stiff with cold. She got on the tire swing and pumped her legs to warm up. Swinging had never been such a chore.

In the forty-eighth, forty-ninth, and fiftieth minutes, she counted how many mushrooms had sprung up in the storm (thirteen) and, while examining one, found three snails with delicate shells the rain turned shiny and dazzling. She kneeled in the wet grass for a closer look. Unlike the small-but-sturdy shells of the purplish periwinkles she stepped on at Sand Beach all the time without worry, these thin yellow swirls offered little protection. They seemed more like dresses than armor.

Lily pictured an escargatoire of field snails gliding and twirling in a tiny ballroom, sticky trails sliming out behind them as they waltzed—verrrrrrry slowly—to the sounds of a cricket orchestra. Maybe when the clock struck midnight, an enchanted Snailderella would turn back into a common slug, leaving behind her glass shell for the lovestruck snail prince to find.

In the sixty-third minute, there was still no sign of Anders, and Lily was fully annoyed. It wasn't his fault she was out here sopping wet, but she couldn't help getting frustrated. Even on nice days, he almost never showed up close to when she did anymore. Lately she had to wait not just minutes but sometimes hours. It had never been that way at the beginning.

In the first week, she hadn't waited for him at all. By the second week, she sometimes did, but only for five or ten minutes. As the months passed, the wait lengthened and lengthened. Now she sometimes worried he might not come at all.

The change was so gradual, she almost didn't see it happen. She almost believed it was all in her head. But the numbers in her notebook proved it.

Anders was slipping away from her, bit by bit. Not only was the overlap shrinking but also, whatever pulled him there in the first place, its pull wasn't as strong.

Except he was pulled there because of her. Like magnets. He'd said so. And if anything, she was pulling him harder, or trying to.

Wasn't she?

She glanced at her watch. Seventy-two minutes. Seventy-two and a half. Seventy-three. But the overlap didn't work in the rain. She was only being stubborn at this point. She was only staying out here to prove it.

She sat on the swing and tried to think of everything she knew about magnets, which, actually, was quite a lot. They'd done a whole unit on them in third grade, and Lily had always loved science.

All magnets had two poles, one north and one south. Opposite poles attracted each other, and like poles pushed apart. The pushing apart was called repulsion. She and Anders were polar opposites, a north/south pair, so they always came together. Even now.

A magnet's force wasn't only contained to its poles, she remembered. The area around a magnet was magnetically charged too. That was called a magnetic field, and magnetic fields came in different sizes. A really strong magnet had a big magnetic field. Weaker magnets had smaller ones.

Magnetic fields were invisible, but in class she'd been able to see one by scattering iron filings onto a piece of cardboard with a magnet placed underneath. When Lily tapped the cardboard, the iron filings jumped into place to show the lines of magnetic force.

Maybe the overlap had invisible currents like that too.

There was an experiment involving a nail and a piece

of wire she magnetized by touching its ends to the poles of a battery. She'd also magnetized a paper clip by running a magnet across it a bunch of times. But it didn't stay magnetic forever. She would have had to recharge it over and over to stop it from becoming a regular paper clip again.

A raindrop dripped into Lily's right ear. She squished it out with her pinkie and sat up straighter.

Maybe that was it. Maybe she was like that paper clip. Something had given her a magnetic charge, which pulled Anders toward her and created the magnetic field around them. But the charge was fading so the magnetic field was shrinking, and she needed to figure out a way to recharge herself.

Maybe she should have gone out in the thunderstorm after all.

But no, that would have been foolish. Whatever magnetized her in the first place, it wasn't a lightning strike or electric shock. It was something connected to when Anders died. She had become a magnet soon after.

She thought of those foggy, awful days around Anders' death. Mostly she remembered her anger. The missing and grieving and disbelief.

She was still angry. She was still grieving. Those both got a little better when she found the overlap and Anders in it, but she wasn't immediately demagnetized by relief or whatever. So getting wicked upset again probably wouldn't solve it.

It did seem, though, like the overlap had appeared because she needed it. So maybe the force that caused it was something more like force of will. Maybe the magnetic energy was mental and emotional.

When Anders died, she was so sad and lost. She just wanted him back. She wanted it so badly, she caused it to happen. Maybe.

She was less sad now, so he showed up less often. But she still needed him. She needed the overlap.

What if, instead of worrying, she refused to let it shrink? What if she didn't accept it, the way she never accepted his death? If she created the overlap in the first place, she ought to be able to keep it going. She just had to concentrate and push back.

For the hundred-third, hundred-fourth, and hundred-fifth through hundred-sixteenth minutes, she focused and wanted and willed it. She gathered all her magnetic charge—all that anger and sadness, confusion and grief, and also her fierce determination—and hurled it at the boundaries, repelling them with her mind. She pushed and pushed and pushed.

She opened her eyes. She was drenched from the rain and panting with exhaustion, but zipping with exhilaration too.

Without Anders there, she couldn't measure where the boundaries were, but it felt like they had budged. It felt like it was working.

She needed Anders to see it.

She needed him to show up.

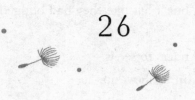

26

The Sun Comes Up

Chirping, singing, whistling birds awakened Lily the next morning. She opened her eyes to sunshine pouring in through the space between the curtains, and her heart swooped and cheered. Finally the rain had stopped. Finally she could see Anders.

She dressed quickly, grabbed the notebook from under her pillow, and ran downstairs. She was so eager and Anders-focused, she didn't notice the smell of pancakes until she'd already entered the kitchen, where Mom was standing at the stove, pouring batter onto the griddle with one hand and holding a spatula in the other. "Good morning," Mom said, almost as chipper as the birds.

Lily stared. "Pancakes?" she said. Her voice lilted up like

it was a question, even though the answer was right there in front of her.

Mom nodded. "It's Sunday. I thought—" Her smile faltered, then recovered. "I thought pancakes would be nice."

"Pancakes are great," Lily rushed to assure her. "I love pancakes." She didn't break into the "It's Sunday! We Get Pancakes! Sunday Pancakes!" song she and Anders used to sing for the occasion, and which always made Mom laugh. It would sound empty and wrong without him. Instead, she gave Mom a quick squeeze from behind and got out the maple syrup.

Mom served them each a warm, buttery plateful, and Lily decorated hers with syrup swirls. She took a huge bite and beamed at Mom, who grinned back around her own mouthful.

The pancakes were delicious. The more Lily ate, the more it felt like things would be okay.

Mom poured a second cup of coffee and nodded at the notebook beside Lily's plate. "What's that for? Are you writing a story?" she asked.

"Nope," Lily said with her mouth full. "I'm recording observations."

"Ooh, about what?" Mom blew on her hot coffee but didn't take a sip. The scent wafted toward Lily, who thought it smelled much nicer than coffee tasted.

She chewed and swallowed another big bite before she

answered. The notebook was hard to explain. "Um, nature and stuff. Things like that."

"Sounds fun." Mom blinked like she'd just remembered something. "Do you want to call and see if Deandra can come over? We can pick her up if her mom brings her home."

"No," Lily said. "No, thank you." She swigged the last of her orange juice and slid off her stool in a hurry. "Actually, I better get going. There's a lot I want to observe today."

"Sure," Mom said, and Lily could tell from the unfocused look in her eyes that her thoughts were already elsewhere.

So were Lily's. She rinsed both their plates, put them in the dishwasher, and ran outside to change the world.

27

Mind Over Matter

It was a humid, buggy day, with the ground still damp in places, so Lily kicked off her sandals to pace the overlap barefoot. She focused better while in motion, and moving around seemed good for both discouraging mosquitoes and encouraging the borders to budge.

By the time Anders appeared, eighty-eight minutes later, Lily was as sweaty and hot as if she'd been pushing a wheelbarrow of bricks. She wiped her face on her T-shirt, marked the time he showed up in her notebook, and turned to him, triumphant. "I figured it out," she said.

"Figured what out?" he asked. He claimed the tire swing and steered it toward a dappled patch of shade.

"How the overlap works! And how to fix it."

Anders frowned slightly. Lily huffed. It was just like him to be skeptical when she got excited.

"Remember the thing we said before about how you're drawn here because of me? How it's like magnets?" she prompted.

He added a squint to his frown. "That's what *you* said before. *I* said I couldn't explain it."

She rolled her eyes, but she was glowing. "Right. Well, I can."

She told him her whole theory about the overlap's magnetic field—about opposite poles attracting, like poles repelling, and magnets sometimes needing to be recharged. How the overlap's magnetism seemed tied to her mind and emotions, which meant *she* was the weakening magnet, but by recharging her emotional currents, she could strengthen and expand the whole thing. She could move the edges outward, if she focused with everything she had. She'd already tried it. She could feel it working.

Anders listened without interrupting. It came out messier and more jumbled than it seemed in her head, and she tripped over several words. She gestured wildly as she talked, and probably looked a little ridiculous, but her arms were as eager as the rest of her—her whole body, jumpy to explain.

The more worked up Lily got, the stiller Anders' face became, which only made Lily more animated. She didn't expect him to mirror her excitement right off—he'd always been the calmer, more cautious twin. He approached ideas slowly and thoughtfully, whereas Lily cannonballed toward them, same as she did with new people or places. (Or at least, as she did before he died. That, too, had shifted.) But she hadn't expected he wouldn't believe her.

His doubt stabbed like a betrayal—like he'd chosen to feel it. Like he *wanted* to abandon her. He'd gotten more and more detached from everything since he died, but this was the first time she felt him detaching from her.

It wasn't his fault, she reminded herself. It was the magnets. Their weakening pull. And she had found a way to fix it. Now that he was here, she could prove it.

"Anyway, you'll see," she said, taking a too-big gulp from her water bottle. Some of the liquid dripped down her chin, onto her shirt. "Come on, let's measure."

Anders shook his head slowly. "No."

"What?" Lily couldn't even process why he'd said that. She wanted to laugh. But it didn't look or sound like a joke.

He sighed. "I said no," he repeated. "I don't want to measure it."

Lily did laugh this time—he was being so incredibly ludicrous—but it sounded more like a strangled choke. It felt that way too. She took a deep breath, and another. "Why not?" she finally managed to say.

"I don't want to keep doing this. I don't want to spend

all our time this way, however much we have left. What's the point?" he said.

"The point?" Lily exploded in disbelief. "The point is to save the overlap so we can spend our time however we want. The point is to stop it from shrinking so I can still see you. The point is to make sure we *don't* run out of time. To fix it. Did you even listen to what I just told you?"

He nodded. "I listened. But it won't work. I mean, it isn't working."

"Argh!" Lily screamed. "What do you even know? How would you know if you won't let me measure?"

"I'm sorry," he said softly. "I can't see the strings. If the boundary moved back, I would see them."

Lily held still and realized how much her arms had been flailing. She gave them a moment to rest. "Not necessarily," she said finally. "Maybe I only pushed the edges back a little, not as far as they moved since we measured. I've only been pushing a couple of hours, but those strings have been there for days. It was raining. You weren't here."

"Lily," he said.

"Just let me measure," she pleaded.

He groaned. "You're obsessed!"

"And you've stopped caring about everything, even this! Even me!" She wanted him to deny it. He didn't.

He shook his head sadly. "You can't control this by wanting it. You can't control *me* that way either. There's not some set of rules and tasks you can follow to make things different. I wish you could. But you can't change this with your mind. You're not Yoda. You're just you."

Lily slumped against the apple tree and the fight whooshed out of her. Most of it. "But you came back when I needed you. You said yourself you're only here because of me. And I still need you. I never stopped," she said.

Anders' eyes brimmed with tears. "I know. But, Lily . . . I might not be able to stay."

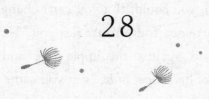

28

The Tangled Web We Weave

L ily stared up into the apple tree, refusing to look at her brother. Refusing to cry. She spotted a spiderweb in the branches and focused on that instead. A spider with striped legs and a big abdomen held still near the web's center, and Lily thought of Charlotte, the brilliant, loyal spider in that book Mom read to her and Anders, and how they all cried when Charlotte died at the end.

Spiders worked quickly and secretively. Lily never saw them weaving, only sitting around looking lazy, or crawling swiftly away. But they built whole elaborate worlds overnight, spun from nothing other than what they had inside them—sticky strings and determination. She couldn't help but admire that.

A mosquito buzzed past her ear with a horrible whine. She swatted and hoped the spider would catch and eat it. She hoped the spider would capture and eat the whole stinking world. Wrap it up, suck its blood, and destroy it all. *The end.* Lily would help. But the spider didn't look like she wanted that.

The ropes of the tire swing creaked beneath Anders' weight. Lily kept her gaze on the spider and wondered if its web caught more than bugs and debris—if the grief, anger, wishes, fear, and disappointment shooting off her might stick to its delicate threads. What would a spider do with all those captured feelings? Could it suck them dry or spin them into something beautiful or dangerous?

She turned to discuss it with Anders and remembered just in time she was too mad at him. She curled her toes in the grass. "So that's it," she said. "You're giving up. And I should let you just slip away."

He grimaced. "I'm not giving up. I'm being realistic."

Now it was Lily's turn to frown.

"Unlike some people, I'm accepting the truth that's in front of me. I don't have a choice in this either, you know," he said.

"But you do! You can choose to help me figure it out! You can choose to try!" Her arms were flapping again. She crossed them. "How come you remember who Yoda is but when I mentioned Ms. Witham the other day, you were like, who?"

He looked at her blankly. Her eyes bugged out. "Our principal? You forgot her again!" she said.

"Sorry," he murmured.

She shook her head. "You see? It's from the magnet not pulling as hard. You're forgetting more. You're invested less. You don't show up for as long or as often. It's like you're pulling away from this world." *And from me*, she thought but didn't say.

Anders stared at the ground like a toddler getting scolded. Lily pictured herself cheering him up with a surprise lollipop, but that wasn't the solution she had. "We need to recharge the magnet to pull you back. Please just try it," she said, with as logical and not-desperate a tone as she could manage.

Even if he refused, she would keep recharging it herself. But she wanted him to try with her. They were stronger and better together. Every magnet had two opposite poles.

"Lily, I don't think you're the magnet," he said.

"Oh yeah? Then what is?" she shot back. He didn't answer. She glanced around, and gasped. "The tire swing!" she said. It wasn't exactly at the center of the overlap, but everything did seem to be shrinking toward it. Maybe he was onto something.

"No, I mean . . ." Anders paused and closed his eyes. Lily waited. He reopened them. "I have a different theory," he said.

She nearly pounced to pull it out of him. It was about time. "What is it?"

He looked at her carefully. "You're not going to like it."

"That's your theory?" she teased.

He didn't smile. "No. That's my theory about the theory."

She sat on the ground, crisscross applesauce. "Just tell me."

He got off the swing and sat facing her, their knees almost touching. Twin opposites. "How long has it been?" he asked.

Lily knew what he meant—he'd asked this before. "Four months, two weeks, and one day," she said. Since he'd died.

He pressed his tongue between his lips and nodded. Lily braced herself. He said it slowly. "We were together for nine months before we were born, right? Like, in the womb?"

"Seven and a half," she said. "We were preemies."

He exhaled. "Okay." She waited for him to continue. He took his time. "So maybe we get seven months or whatever together after too. Like before we were born, but in reverse."

She didn't move. She couldn't.

"Before, in the womb, we both grew. Now I'm doing the opposite," he said, like it wasn't the most devastating thought in the world.

She jolted. "You're not shrinking," she protested. He hadn't grown more, like she had, but he was still the same size as when he died.

He shrugged. "No, but the space we share is. And like you said, I'm here less and less. I remember less of anything that isn't you."

Her heart shrieked at every piece of her brain that thought this sounded possible. She wouldn't have it. "But why?" she said, stalling. "What's the point?"

He considered that. "I don't know. Maybe we spent those first months becoming who we are together, and now we get these extra months to become who we'll be apart."

Lily's head snapped up. "There's no me without you," she said.

"There hasn't been. But there will be," he said.

He was so calm. She wanted to shake him. "Will there be a you without me?" she asked. It sounded like a challenge.

He lifted one shoulder. "Maybe yes. Not exactly. And not here. Not like I was."

They sat in silence for a minute. She snorted, though nothing was funny. "You're right," she said. "I hate it."

His mouth twisted. She knew that smile. It dammed up tears.

"What happens when the seven and a half months are over?" she asked.

"I don't know," he said. "I guess we'll find out."

She dug her fingernails into the ground. "I don't want to," she said.

He nodded. "I know."

He shifted, and she knew there was more. "What?" she pushed.

"Nothing. Just . . . what were you going to do, live here forever and spend all your time with me? Not hang out with anyone else? Like, ever?"

She glared at him. "Yes." That had been her plan. And she didn't think there was anything wrong with it.

But if Anders was right—if his theory proved true—she was going to need a plan B.

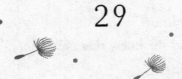

29

Countdown

In her room after dark, Lily tuned in to the ball game, shoved her notebook into a drawer, opened a graphic novel on her lap, and tried to think about anything other than the overlap. It was hard.

Very hard.

The DH stepped up to bat and the runner took a lead off first, and the count was one and one, two and one, two and two, and if Anders was right, they had only three months left.

Three months.

Who knew how much he would even be around in that time. How long before he barely remembered her?

A fly ball to the left went foul behind the pole, and the

count stayed two and two. In the pen, a new relief pitcher began warming up, and it was jarring that Lily didn't know who he was. She'd barely paid attention to baseball this season. She didn't even know how her favorite players were doing. She must have missed a trade.

Of course she had. She hardly knew about anything that went on outside the overlap. Anders wasn't the only one who'd stopped caring about the rest of the world.

Most of it.

A line drive up the middle went straight to the center fielder's glove and the runner got tagged out at second; double play. The side retired.

Seventh inning stretch.

Lily shifted on her bed. She was antsy and itchy. Whether she cared about the world or not, she lived in it. And Anders didn't.

She stood. The book, which she'd forgotten, fell to the floor and clunked under the bed. She ignored it and shook out her limbs, two at a time, like her third-grade teacher had them do when the class was too wiggly to focus. Jiggling her arms and legs helped, but it wasn't enough. She wanted to run around, run this off—to bolt out the door and keep going forever. Maybe she would run until she forgot everything and everyone too.

She put a hand on the doorknob, then dropped it.

Even if that were possible, she couldn't leave Mom.

Besides, the moon wasn't bright enough tonight to light her way. She would have to get a flashlight, make sure the batteries worked, and carry extras for when the light dimmed but her sadness kept going. There weren't enough batteries in the world to outlast that.

Why bother.

She probably couldn't even run as far as the bridge.

Maybe Mom would be up for movie night, and Lily could curl against her and be less jittery. Movies were usually good distractions, and Mom was always nice to lean on. They could share a blanket and a bowl of popcorn, like they had watching *Shrek* last week, and she would choose something funny so Mom wouldn't cry.

But it was pretty late for starting a movie, and even funny movies had sad parts. Some had a lot. Lily never noticed that before Anders died and suddenly everything in her life had sad parts too. Even the happy things contained sadness because they happened without him alive, which he never would be, ever again, and no amount of being sad could change that. Not that she wanted to stop being sad and just go on all happy without him.

There was no solution to the problem of grief. There was only living it.

She turned off the radio even though the game was mid-pitch. It wasn't making her any less restless.

Sometimes Lily's grief was a shadow or a cloud. It

hovered over her shoulder. It lingered off to the side. Other times it was a rock, firm and heavy on her chest. It wrapped itself around her or sank into her bones. She was getting used to how grief shape-shifted—the ways it showed up like new, or as it had before—sometimes shouting everything else out, sometimes humming quietly beneath it.

No matter its form, the grief was always there. It was almost a way of keeping Anders with her. Like a new form of love, but painful.

Tonight the grief was fidgety. It didn't want to be ignored. It was jumpy with fear she might lose him again.

Not might: *would*.

What form would grief take then?

Lily collapsed. It was too much. She couldn't stand it.

She curled up with the blankets pulled over her head, and let darkness swallow her completely.

30

The Unfair Grounds

She didn't remember falling asleep. Perhaps that was what made her dream so real.

The Blue Hill fairgrounds were as dusty and crowded as at the end of every summer—filled with music and lights; lines for flashing, swirling rides; stray red tickets and ketchup-streaked food trays; game booths lined with stuffed animals, inflatable dinosaurs, rubber bracelets, and funny hats; food stands offering caramel apples, frozen lemonade, and—her favorite—dough boys coated with powdered sugar and cinnamon. Lily wandered through it, feeling lost. No, not lost, but like she was missing something. Missing someone. Only partly even there herself.

She wove around overflowing trash cans and endless strangers—people laughing, crying, shouting, talking; none of whom seemed to see her—past the rides and games, to the far end of the fair: the livestock exhibits where sheep, goats, pigs, cows, horses, and rabbits hung out in hay-lined stalls they'd made their homes for the weekend. It was quieter here than at the rest of the fair, and being near the animals calmed her. Her sight got clearer and her mind more focused, and she realized who she was missing right as she found him. Anders. There he was, next to a pen with three lambs. He took her hand and they explored the whole fair together.

She woke up smiling, still delighted at the Ferris wheel, the fireworks, the enormous blue cotton candy they'd shared. Still relieved and content to have found him. Looking forward to being together today.

Seconds later, the truth crashed down like a wave and knocked the air clean out of her. She grasped her chest. It hurt to breathe. It hurt to live. The pain of losing her brother cut sharp, new, and deep as he was ripped away from her all over again and dragged off in the undertow.

It was just so horribly unfair.

Lily rolled onto her side, hugged her knees to her chest, and squeezed as hard as she could for as long as she could. The stabs dulled to a raw ache. Her ragged breaths smoothed out to normal. She felt drained. Hopeless. Empty.

She held still for a long time, until all she felt was nothing.

She heard birds outside and a truck coming over the hill, and her retinas registered sunlight. It was another perfect, awful summer day. Maybe she would close her eyes and skip it.

A noise in the next room made her muscles tense. She held her breath and listened for what surely she'd misheard—but no, there it was again. She pressed her ear, slowly, cautiously, to the wall between her room and Anders'. It was impossible, but she heard him. He was home. He was here.

She jumped out of bed and flew from her room into his. "Hey!" she said, her voice full joy, to the back of him, half submerged in the closet where he was rummaging. "What are you— Oh." The question dropped and her euphoria plummeted. Her heartbeat pounded in her ears and berated her from inside, pulsing *stupid, stupid, stupid.*

It wasn't Anders. It was Mom.

Mom backed out of the closet and stood to her full height. In one hand she held Anders' sneaker, a twin without its pair. She looked almost as startled as Lily. "Sorry. I hope I didn't wake you," Mom said.

Lily shook her head but didn't speak. She'd seen Mom

in Anders' room before, but only crying and sitting on his bed. Never taking things from his closet. Never making her think she was he.

She noticed boxes on the floor and one on Anders' desk. She saw Anders' clothes and possessions inside them, but could not process why they were there. His things shouldn't be in boxes. That wasn't where they belonged.

She stepped toward one, pulled Anders' baseball glove out of it, and slipped her fingers inside. It was stiff from disuse and needed to be oiled. Hers probably did too. She would oil them both, tie them into shape, and sleep with them under her mattress tonight. They usually broke in their gloves in April, to be ready for the first toss of summer. She'd forgotten this year. She would make up for it.

"That box is for things I thought we might keep," Mom said nonsensically.

The glove felt heavy and awkward on Lily's left hand—her throwing side. Anders was right-handed, her mirror opposite. Her fingers were a little longer and his palms a little wider, but the glove still fit. It was grimy inside with dried sweat and grit from last summer, when he'd daydreamed in the outfield, watching butterflies and drawing patterns in the dirt with his foot, while Lily played shortstop. Her throwing arm hurled bullets. He'd only signed up for Little League because she did.

"Of course, if I've put anything you want into the give-away boxes, feel free to take it out," Mom said. "Some of it, it's hard to decide. Even harder than I expected. This is just a preliminary sorting."

Lily pulled off the glove. Horror bloomed inside her. "You're giving his stuff away?" She stared at the open drawers, half-empty shelves, and stripped bed. Last time she'd been in here, everything was as Anders had left it. Now Mom was packing him away, piece by piece, into cardboard coffins. "What are you doing?" she yelled. She ran to the nearest box, dumped everything out, and scrambled to put it all back where it belonged. Did the school spelling bee trophy go on his desk or did he keep that on the shelf behind it? Was the sparkly pencil topper even his, or had he borrowed that from her and never returned it? She tried not to hyperventilate, but already the task felt impossible. Like all the king's horses and all the king's men, she couldn't put Anders together again.

She whirled around to face Mom, who still stood there holding one sneaker. "You're getting rid of him!" Lily screamed. "You're throwing away the only pieces we have left!" She choked on her words and coughed. A sob heaved through her lungs but wouldn't come out. She wished she could cry, but her tears got burned up by rage.

"Lily," Mom said, her voice gentle and soft, like she was

soothing a wild beast. Lily snarled. "We're not throwing anything out—or even giving it away yet. I'm just sorting things, and getting used to the idea of sharing the stuff we don't need. Spreading it, like seeds. Don't you think he would like that?"

Lily swallowed hard. Anders had always been more generous with his belongings than she was, and he probably didn't remember he owned half these things. He wouldn't miss them. But she would.

"These objects aren't Anders. They're just things. We will always have him with us," Mom said, and pressed her hand to her heart. The other hand finally put down the sneaker. Lily blinked as Mom moved closer. She let herself be wrapped in a hug.

"But . . . why?" she said into Mom's shirt. It was soft and smelled faintly of lavender and pine, like the homemade sachets Mom kept in her drawers and the pillows she sold online and at craft fairs.

Mom stroked Lily's back in small, soothing circles. Lily wondered if Mom was so good at petting because of the years she had Barkly. "Lorelei says Anders is worried we're getting stuck in our grief. He wants us to live fully and make space for more joy. She thought cleaning his room might be a good start. He's continuing on his journey. He wants us to continue on ours."

Lily yanked herself out of the hug. "*Lorelei* says? The psychic fraud? You're clearing out his room because of her?"

"Not because of her," Mom said. "For us."

But Lily wasn't listening. She was too horrified. She was too over this. She whipped around and ran from the room, from the house, from her mom. She ran to the overlap and waited.

31

Ripped to Pieces

I t was a long wait, and Lily really needed to pee.

She'd gone straight from her bed to Anders' room to the overlap, without even brushing her teeth or changing out of pajamas, and she regretted not using the bathroom or grabbing breakfast on her way out. She ignored her screaming bladder and tried to focus on nudging the boundaries—in case he was wrong; in case she *could* move them—but it was difficult to concentrate when she was worried she might explode.

She ran into the woods and crouched to pee on the mossy ground, hoping if Anders appeared in that moment he would at least be facing the other direction. She half expected that getting in such an embarrassing position would summon him. It didn't.

Peeing helped, but there wasn't much she could do about her grumbling stomach and sour mouth, or the fact that she was also really thirsty. She waited it out as long as she could, then slunk back inside to get food and put on real clothes.

Lily moved quietly in the kitchen and crept up the stairs, light-footed and stealthy like a fox. The last thing she wanted was to talk more with Mom or, worse, be asked to help put things in boxes. But if Mom heard she was there, she gave Lily space—and Lily certainly didn't look into Anders' room. She put on shorts, fetched her notebook and watch, and returned outside to wait as long as it took.

When she and Anders were bored, they liked to play a game called statues, where the point was to strike a pose and go completely motionless, as if they'd been turned to stone. Whoever moved first lost. Anders was ridiculously good at it, like maybe he'd been made of granite in a past life. Lily tended to get itchy or start laughing, or choose too ambitious a position—one that looked cool but was impossible to hold for multiple minutes. She'd always been impatient and bad at staying in place.

It was just her luck that now she had to wait around all the time. If Anders were the one to have long waits for her in the overlap, he would probably barely notice. He would just daydream the time away.

Lily scratched a bug bite on her shin and pressed an X into the bump to release the itch. It was a trick she'd learned from Mom, who learned it from Lily's great-grandmother—Mom's grandmother, who raised her—and although Lily wasn't completely convinced it worked, she liked that it was passed from Mimi to Mom to her (though Mom said there were fewer mosquitoes in Boston). Lily definitely would have liked Mimi, who was a Red Sox fan and a marine biologist, loved chocolate and ordering takeout, wore lots of purple, and lived in a tall house in the city. Lily and Anders never got to meet her—she died a few months before they were born—but Mom had told them many stories, including how Lily was named for Mimi—or rather, for the scent of her favorite perfume.

Anders got his name because Mom thought it sounded nice with Lily's and knew that as twins, their names would often be linked. Often, but not always.

Lily tried not to think of the not always.

If her great-grandmother hadn't died, Lily would have been a city kid like Mom. That was pretty strange to imagine—growing up with sidewalks, subways, and skyscrapers instead of the field and spruce trees and tides. But Mimi did die, and Mom sold the house in Boston, bought a farmhouse in Maine, and moved there to sew quilts and raise her twins.

Lily closed her eyes and gave the borders a shove. When she opened them, she saw Anders in the field, picking daisies and linking their stems. She jotted down the time and got up to join him.

"Daisy killer," she said, hoping he would remember.

He smirked. "Making a crown is entirely different from ripping a flower to pieces," he informed her.

"Is it, though?" she said. It was a comfort to revisit an old, familiar joke.

Years ago, she stood in this field and pulled petals off a daisy, chanting, "He loves me, he loves me not." (She didn't even know who "he" was. It was just a game Deandra had taught her.) When Anders saw it, he burst into tears, ran to the house, and told Mom she was a flower killer. She'd teased him about it for ages but never treated a daisy that way again.

"Yes," he said, and placed the flower crown on her head. She stood taller.

"What's the difference between picking petals and blowing the seeds off a dandelion? How come that's okay?" she asked, still defending her honor.

"Dandelion seeds *want* to be blown. It helps them spread. Duh," he said.

"Oh." She put a hand to the crown to stop it from sliding. "Right." She pictured Mom holding a box of Anders' things and blowing them into the wind, making a wish as they scattered.

She imagined a single puff of breath sending her heart in a million directions. The shards would spread and land and grow new hearts to bloom and hope and ache.

"Mom wants us to give away your stuff," she announced. She watched his face. No reaction. "She's packing your room into boxes."

"Okay," he said.

"Okay?" she repeated.

"Sure, why not. It's not like I'm going to use it."

"Hmph." Lily took off the crown and examined its flowers. It was late in the season for daisies. This might be the last flower crown he would make.

"So is Mom doing a little better, then?" he asked. She looked up, confused, so he explained. "Getting rid of my things sounds better than sleeping all day and crying."

Lily considered that. "She is and she isn't," she said. "And it was Lorelei the Psychic Fraud's idea to clear out your room. She says you want us to 'make space for joy' or something stupid like that."

He wrinkled his nose. "Oh."

"Yeah."

"I mean, I do want you to be happy and move on or whatever," he added.

"Anders!" She jerked her hands in protest and the daisies went flying.

He ducked as the crown nearly hit him. "What?"

"I'm not moving on from you. I'm never *moving on* from this," she said. "Your death isn't something for me to get over."

He sighed. "Yeah, but you can't be sad every day forever. Not as sad as you started. Not as sad as you are now. Mom can't stay in bed and you can't just hang out here with me. You have lives to live and places to be and friends to—"

"I don't have any friends," she interrupted.

"Sure you do," he said.

"Nope."

"You have Quinn," he pointed out.

"True," she conceded. "Except she's in high school. We're only hanging out because it's summer. I don't have any friends who go to my school and are close to my age and aren't chickens." She missed the chickens. She wished she could pet Henrietta and Pearl right now. She wanted to coo back at Frankie, and let Big Bertha peck her shoelaces, and give extra special scraps to Achoo and Snowball. She'd stayed away for so long—two whole weeks—she wondered if they even remembered her. She had no idea how long chickens' memories lasted.

His eyebrows pushed together. "What about . . .

what's-her-name? You know, with the freckles? That girl. Your best friend?"

Lily savored a flash of pleasure that he'd forgotten her. "Deandra?" she said.

He brightened. "Yeah."

She shrugged. "I'm not talking to her." She made a point of sounding like she didn't care, but it pinched a little, just saying it.

He tilted his head. "Since when?"

"Since our birthday."

"Oh." He looked sheepish. "Did I know that?"

Now she felt bad. "No. I didn't tell you."

His shoulders relaxed. "Do you want to?"

She spilled it all out—the awful thing Deandra said; the horrid, gleeful way she'd said it; how unbearably obnoxious and off-putting she had seemed ever since. Anders listened to the whole thing without interrupting. When she finished, he kept listening, as though waiting for more.

She lifted her eyebrows to prompt him. He blinked. "She was right though," he said finally. "I did die."

Lily reeled. "That's not the point!" She couldn't believe Anders, of all people, didn't get it.

He gave her a concerned look. "So who are you friends with now?" he asked.

"No one! I just told you." She crossed her arms. This

kept getting worse and worse. What good was a twin who refused to understand her?

Anders sat in the tall grass, so she sat too. He picked a stalk with a feathery top and chewed the smooth end, looking thoughtful. She picked a stalk of her own, bit down, and let it hang out of her mouth. He wiggled his nose like a rabbit. Her anxiety loosened a smidge.

She glanced at the boundary string pinned several feet away, and wondered—hoped—but decided not to ask. He would tell her if he could see it. He knew it was important. And she didn't want another lecture or letdown.

Anders nibbled the grass. "What about Kenny?" he asked.

"What about him?"

"He's a good friend."

"He's *your* friend," she said.

He shrugged. "He likes you too."

"He does?"

"Yeah."

Lily tried to think of a time when she and Kenny interacted without Anders. She couldn't come up with one. But he was a doer, not a talker. And he'd always been nice. "I saw him at Burnt Cove the other day and ignored him," she admitted. "Him and his dad and Marlaina."

"I don't think he'll hold it against you. Next time, say hi."

"Okay," she said.

"Promise?"

"Promise."

"Good. It's not right for me to be the only one you talk to," he said.

She glared. "Even if I had a million friends, no one could replace you."

Anders laughed.

"What?" Lily said.

He shook his head. "Nothing. You're just being a dingus."

"Thanks a lot."

"You're welcome," he said, and blew his grass at her. It didn't go very far. "No one could replace you either. Dingus."

She'd known it was true, but hearing it helped. Anders always knew how to make her feel better.

She would never have another friend like him.

32

An Unwelcome Offer

Lily walked up the hill to Ms. Turner's the next morning, and was relieved to find the chickens did remember her. Henrietta and Big Bertha ran right over, and when Lily sat to pet them, Snowball invited herself onto Lily's lap.

Frankie was wary and kept her distance at first, like maybe she didn't forgive Lily for not coming around in so long. But Ms. Turner let her feed the girls some lettuce she'd saved, and that seemed to win Frankie back. She even rubbed her head against Lily's knee before Lily got up to end the long visit. Lily promised to come back soon.

On the way down the hill, she waved to Quinn, who was biking in the opposite direction. Quinn pulled off the road. "You busy?" she asked.

"Just walking home."

"Want to go to Aunt Linda's and stack firewood?"

"By myself?" Lily said.

Quinn laughed. "No, with me. I'm not *that* much of a Tom Sawyer. I'll do the work too."

Lily was tempted, but she'd already spent the whole morning with the chickens. She couldn't skip out on Anders in the afternoon too. If he was right, they had only a few months left, and she couldn't afford to waste a day of it. "I can't," she said. "I have to do some chores for my mom." She resolved to get the mail on her way inside and straighten her room later so this wouldn't be purely a fib. "Will you be doing it again tomorrow? I could probably help out then."

"Definitely," Quinn said. "It's a lot of wood. Enough to heat the house all winter. The woodstove's her only heat source. My dad keeps trying to convince her to get oil heat or electric, so she doesn't have to worry about keeping the stove going all night, but she says it's too expensive. When you pee at her house in January, the toilet seat is freezing."

"Good to know," Lily said. They agreed Quinn would stop by on her way to Aunt Linda's the next morning, and Lily would help for a couple hours before visiting the chickens on her way back. It felt good to have a plan other than waiting by herself in the overlap.

At the top of the next hill, she opened the mailbox. There were two envelopes and a seed catalog inside. She grabbed them, crossed the street, and flipped through the catalog as she made her way up to the house. Mom didn't garden the way Ms. Turner did, but the photos of flowers and plants were so pretty, it seemed a shame to throw the catalog away. Maybe instead of recycling it, she would cut it up and make a collage. Or she could tape some of the flowers around the frame of her bulletin board, the way Quinn's mirror was surrounded by photos. That would look pretty and colorful. She would try it.

She dropped the envelopes on the counter for Mom to see, and was about to go back to the catalog, when she noticed her name on the top one. Not just her name: Anders' too. It was addressed to "Lily Anders," as if a single person with those two names lived at this address on South Deer Isle Road.

Lily frowned and picked up the letter cautiously, though she knew the typo wouldn't bite her. She wasn't sure who would write to them like that, even by mistake. Everyone who knew her also knew that Anders was dead.

She slid her finger under the flap. *Dear Ms. Anders*, the letter read. *Congratulations! You have been preselected for this special offer of a QuickDollar Fun Cash SilverClub Credit Card with 0% interest applied to all purchases made within the first six months! To accept this exclusive, limited-time offer, simply—*

The words swarmed on the page like a cloud of blackflies

and Lily couldn't read any further. She placed the letter on the counter, but it slipped to the floor. She felt too heavy and empty to get it.

Her lightness and joy from spending time with the chickens and Quinn had been flattened like a pancake run over by a tractor trailer. As she stood there and blinked, she filled up with rage, as though she were a glass held under a faucet of fury. It had almost reached the top.

If she didn't move quickly, the fury would spill over. It would flow out of her and keep going and going until everyone and everything drowned.

She bent to pick up the letter and heard Quinn's voice in her head. *You know, sometimes it helps to tell someone what you're feeling.* She remembered Ms. Weed's not-so-subtle encouragement when she'd given Lily the notebook. *It's good to have a safe place to write things down.* And Anders, sticking his nose in things. *It's not right for me to be the only one you talk to.*

Hmph. They wanted her to say how she felt? Fine. She flipped over the letter and took out her green pen.

To Whom It May Concern, she wrote on the back in her neatest, most serious handwriting. *I am eleven years old and I don't need a credit card. My brother, Anders, died in March so he doesn't need one either. You shouldn't be offering credit cards to eleven-year-olds anyway. And if you're going to send someone a letter, you should be careful to get their name right and make sure they are not dead. I do not want your special offer. Sincerely, Lily*

She folded the paper, put it inside the return envelope that was already addressed and stamped, and sealed it. There.

Maybe it wasn't exactly what Anders and Quinn had meant, but she did feel a little bit better.

33

Less and Less

Without discussing it, Lily and Quinn fell into a new routine for August. Quinn stopped at Lily's house on her bike most mornings. They walked up the hill to say hello to the chickens, and if Quinn's chore for the day at Aunt Linda's was something fun, like stacking wood or picking vegetables or painting the old shed, Lily stayed and helped awhile before spending the afternoon in the overlap. If Quinn's chore for the day was something not fun, like vacuuming or dusting or organizing Aunt Linda's spices, Lily and the chickens had an extra-long visit, because Anders had stopped appearing before lunchtime.

Mom was appearing at lunchtime though. Most days, right around when Lily got home, she wandered into the kitchen to make sandwiches, which the two of them ate together.

Mom was cautious and gentle around Lily now, as if she were a bird who'd landed unexpectedly close, and Mom was afraid she might startle and fly off. Lily didn't see Mom do any *actual* tiptoeing, but her words and movements were light and soft, reminding Lily of that phrase, to "tiptoe around" something. Neither of them brought up the boxes, the psychic, or the fight. They didn't say Anders' name even once.

At first, Lily was relieved, but soon she started to hate it. The more they didn't talk about Anders, the more it felt like she couldn't or shouldn't.

This was different from the weeks after he died, when she tried not to mention him and risk making Mom cry— the few moments when she wasn't crying already. It was different from when Mom started sobbing less but staring into space more, as if watching a memory of him in the distance. Those times were awful, but at least Anders was part of them.

Now, it felt like Mom had carefully boxed him up and tucked him away. She no longer cried in front of Lily (though her puffy eyes revealed she cried plenty in private). She didn't reference him in little ways, like calling it the Other Lily's Pond or making Sunday pancakes. Anders became a topic Mom actively avoided, and the longer this went on, the emptier the house seemed without him. The more days that passed where he didn't come up, the more it felt like they'd deleted or erased him.

Lily tried to discuss it with Anders, but she felt lonely in that too. He listened while she rambled but didn't give ideas on how to fix it or offer more than a "that stinks." She wondered if he could even really picture it. She wondered when he'd stopped feeling what she felt.

It was getting harder to engage him with anything other than the right here, right now. He seemed more and more detached from everything outside the overlap, even Mom. Whatever hold on him the world had, he'd slipped away from it almost completely.

They played more and talked less. Hitting a croquet ball or building a fairy house was simpler than making conversation with someone who was only partly there. Lily couldn't stand the reminder that he was slipping away from her too.

But he was. She kept pushing the boundaries with all her might, but even without measuring, she saw it wasn't working. Anders moved within a smaller and smaller area. He showed up less often and disappeared sooner. A few times, when she glanced at him, he didn't appear to be solid.

Dusk fell earlier. Nights cooled faster. She was spending less time with her brother than she was with the chickens and Quinn. When she mentioned that fact to him, he only nodded and gave a quick shrug. Like that was inevitable. Like it was okay.

The evening shadows across the field came sooner and stretched farther. The start of school barreled toward her like a bus without brakes.

Summer was almost over and wishing season was nearly gone. In three weeks, she would be a sixth grader, and Anders would not. Lily was so scared of whatever came next, but she couldn't stop time from hurtling forward.

Already it had been five months since he died. Sometimes she wondered if it hurt slightly less or if she'd only gotten used to the pain. Other times it hurt more than ever before and she wondered how she would survive without him.

She put away the notebook and stopped taking it out. She left her watch on the nightstand. She tried to live in the here and now.

He was still here, for now.

34

Bawks and Betrayal

"How come Snowball is the only chicken who likes me?" Quinn complained as they sat in the shade of Ms. Turner's shed to cool off from the walk up the hill. Ten feet away, in his own patch of shade between two bushes with pink flowers, Prince the cat flicked his tail and deliberately ignored them. All six chickens were close by and clucking, but much closer to Lily than Quinn. Quinn reached out to touch Frankie's mottled brown feathers. Frankie dodged her and scuttled away.

"Snowball is the cuddliest chicken; that's true. But she's not the only one who likes you," Lily said. "The others just get skittish if you move too fast or unpredictably. You're a little jumpy for them sometimes, maybe. Like when you jiggle your knee and stuff. You have to be patient." She made a smooth and gentle stroke across Henrietta's back, to demonstrate how the chickens liked it. Henrietta wriggled with pleasure and pushed against Lily's hand to encourage more petting. Frankie made a jealous cluck and hovered nearby. "And Frankie doesn't really trust anyone all that much," she said.

"Except you," Quinn countered. Lily smiled because it was true. She was proud to be Frankie's favorite. "What is it you love about them?" Quinn asked.

Lily shrugged. "I don't know. I just do. They're silly and funny and I like being around them. I've always loved animals. I love how they're so completely themselves." She paused. "Though if I could have any kind of pet, I'd choose a dog."

"Me too. I'd want a scruffy little mutt who acts like she can beat up anyone ten times her size, but who's smart and loyal and sweet at her core," Quinn said.

"I'd love any kind of dog," Lily said. "I've never met a dog I don't like."

"See, I'm like Frankie. Much more discerning. With humans too," Quinn declared.

Henrietta wandered off after a grub and Lily switched to petting Big Bertha, who apparently once was a large, fluffy chick but, full-grown, was about the same size as the others. "Why do you hang out with me?" she asked. She said it as a joke, but secretly hoped Quinn would give a real answer. She loved being Quinn's friend even more than she loved all six chickens. Quinn had made the saddest summer of all time also fun. Lily didn't know what she'd have done without her.

"You're my kind of weirdo," Quinn said. "Plus it's the best way to earn points by far." She pulled her paint-splattered tank top away from her belly and fanned herself with it. Lily watched and felt slightly dizzy.

"What do you mean?" she asked.

"For driving," Quinn said. "I get ten points each time we hang out. Or double points if we do chores. Whichever's more." Her tone was as easy as if she were reporting what kind of cereal she had for breakfast, but the more she talked, the harder it got for Lily to breathe. She felt like she might pass out.

"You're getting *paid* to hang out with me? I'm one of your *chores*?" Her face burned with humiliation, but at least the anger cleared her head.

"Yeah," Quinn said. "I mean, no. Lily, I— Wait."

But Lily didn't hear another word. She scrambled to her feet, grabbed her backpack, and ran.

35

Swarm of Regret

L ily lay on her back in the center of the overlap and stared at the sky without seeing it. A hive of bees had burst from her heart and was swarming and buzzing under her skin, desperate to find an escape. She wished she could open her mouth to let them fly out, and release herself from this horrid embarrassment. But the bees were trapped inside. Lily couldn't do anything about them.

Ten points each time we hang out.

The truth stung.

Lily listed her humiliations, stirring up the bees with each one.

She had thought Quinn actually liked her. She had actually thought they were friends.

She had thought they hung out because it was fun and it was summertime and they found each other interesting. Because she was good at making Quinn laugh.

She'd believed Quinn cared about the stuff Lily told her.

She'd believed Quinn cared about *her*.

She had trusted her.

She should have known.

Quinn was probably laughing right now about how pathetic Lily was.

Worse: She'd probably moved on and forgotten her already, except for the points she would collect for this morning. Ten points for the chore of hanging around with a ridiculous kid.

Grass tickled Lily's calves and an ant crawled down her shin, but she didn't move. She let her weight sink into the ground and wished it would swallow her whole.

The bees settled a bit. They'd get worked up again at the slightest thought of Quinn, so she tried to focus on something else and not agitate them. She looked for shapes in the clouds, though they were mostly just wisps. She listened to the birds and insects.

She felt Anders appear before she saw him—felt his calm. Felt less alone.

He sat in the grass a few feet behind her, whittling a bright green leaf. They didn't speak. She didn't need to. It was enough to have him near.

She held still a while longer, until the bees flew away. She released her breath with the last one and sat up. Anders' leaf was shaped like a duck now. She smiled.

He disappeared at the same instant Lily registered a new sound—someone calling her name. An intruder coming toward them. She whipped around and her smile faded. It was Quinn.

"Hey," Quinn said. Lily glared. "Your mom said you were probably back here and I could—"

"What do you want," Lily snapped. She didn't lift her voice at the end. It wasn't a real question.

Quinn sighed and looked at her sadly, the way one might look at an injured bird. A few more bees erupted from Lily's heart. She didn't want or need Quinn's pity.

"I want to apologize. And to check if you're okay," Quinn said.

Lily flinched. "I'm fine."

Quinn didn't look like she believed it.

Lily picked at a recent scab on her knee. A drop of blood swelled to the surface and glistened in the sun. She stared at it and waited for Quinn to take the hint and walk away.

Quinn moved closer. "Lily, I'm sorry. I really messed up. I should have told you about the points. I don't know why I didn't. I should have told you straight up you'd be helping me out, and asked if you would do me that favor."

Lily looked up. "What favor?"

"The favor of hanging out with me. Helping me earn points. Being my friend."

Lily shook her head. She poked the blood droplet with her pinkie and it smeared. "I thought you liked me," she said, though it was embarrassing to admit.

Quinn laughed, but not meanly. "Of course I like you. Are you kidding? You've been the best part of my summer by far."

Lily blinked at her, disbelieving. Still braced for another trick. "Really?"

"Yes! Hanging with you is way more fun than fishing trash out of a pond."

"But you only spent time with me because you got paid," she said.

"No," Quinn said firmly. "Not at all. And I'm really, really sorry it sounded that way. Plus I'm sorry, like I said, that I hadn't told you. But I promise I never would have spent all that time with you if we weren't friends. There are plenty of other ways to earn points. I could have just spent my days dusting Aunt Linda's porcelain cat figurines."

Lily allowed her a tiny smile. "She does have an impressive collection," she said.

Quinn grinned back and sat in a patch of clover. "I told my mom that I saw you that first day at the pond, and she suggested I take you with me to Ms. Turner's," she said. "I think she just figured . . . maybe you could use a friend. And she knew I liked you. So it seemed like a win-win." Quinn held her gaze. "I'm sorry if I made you feel like a loser."

Lily grimaced. "Yeah. You did," she said. Quinn nodded and looked sad. "But I guess that was nice of your mom. And I'm glad you explained it. I feel a little less horrible now, I think."

Quinn exhaled. "Well, that's a start." She leaned back on her elbows, and Lily did the same. Where before there were bees, things felt warm and loose inside her. Like the bees had left some honey, which was melting in the sun.

It was weird being in the overlap with someone who wasn't Anders. Weird but okay, she decided. Maybe because without him there, it wasn't the overlap. It was part of Lily's field. And it was nice to share the field with a friend on a summer day.

36

Secrets Wrapped and Secrets Hidden

L ily walked past the open door to Anders' room—what used to be *their* room when they were babies with side-by-side cribs, though Lily only remembered that from photos—and did not look inside. She focused instead on the gray floorboards beneath the blue flowered wallpaper that had been there since before they moved in, and made her way to the bathroom to brush her teeth before bed.

Once upon a time, Mom reminded them about toothbrushing, and leaned down for an extra kiss and sniff at tuck-in some nights to check. Now Lily could never brush her teeth again and Mom probably wouldn't say a word about it—not even when they turned mossy green and fell out all at once, costing the tooth fairy a fortune. She had stopped checking Lily's oral hygiene when Anders got sick.

If he hadn't gotten sick, she would have stopped checking eventually. Did teenagers' moms sniff their breath for toothpaste? Did twenty-year-olds reassure their parents, "Yes, I flossed"? Lily wasn't sure. She hadn't been a teenager or a twenty-year-old yet.

She rinsed out her mouth and looked in the mirror. At almost eleven and a half, she was already many months older than Anders ever would be. Their whole lives, she'd been fourteen minutes younger. But her older brother would never get old.

The missing him tightened around her like a lasso and tugged. It pulled her toward his doorway. She steeled herself and peeked inside.

She'd been avoiding his room since the fight with Mom, afraid to see it all packed up. She expected dusty shelves, empty drawers, and stacks of taped-up boxes. Maybe even tumbleweeds blowing through, like in a GIF of the desert. But if anything had been moved in the weeks since she stormed out, she couldn't see it. It was different from how Anders kept it, but that was less shocking the second time around.

There was his baseball glove, on the bed where she'd left it. She stepped inside, picked it up, and hugged it to her chest. She would keep it, for sure. It might be useful for playing catch with someone who came over without a glove—maybe Kenny someday, or Quinn. She put it back in the "keep" box.

The spelling bee trophy could probably go. Actually, most of what Mom had in the box Lily dumped was stuff Anders would have gotten rid of himself in the next major cleaning. She placed those things back in a giveaway box. Like Mom said, they were just objects.

She moved around the room, peering into boxes, touching his things. There was plenty of random stuff she could let go of, actually. The whole place didn't need to be an Anders museum. It wouldn't suit him to be frozen in time. But whatever they used this room for next, it should always hold reminders of him—at least one special shelf for his favorite books and toys, things he'd made, and whatever held the best memories. She set aside an origami flower he'd folded, which definitely belonged on display.

She hoped it wasn't a bad sign that Mom had abandoned the sorting. Anders was right: They didn't want her to be this sad forever. There was relief in the moments when Mom seemed like Mom again—not exactly the same as before Anders died, but closer than when she'd been completely consumed by grief.

At first, Mom's grief was like a coating or a shell—nothing could get past it, in or out. Now it was seeping in to be part of her core. Lily felt that in her own body too.

If Lorelei the Psychic Fraud was even a little bit right

that giving away some of Anders' things could help Mom heal—well, Lily could support that. It wouldn't be all bad. Moving forward wasn't the same as moving on.

Most of Anders' stuffed animals had already gone to other homes a year ago, but Lily spotted Maude—the not-quite-identical twin to her own teddy bear, Bluebeary—peeking out from the closet and grabbed her. Maude could live in Lily's room. With her slightly matted fur specked with glitter glue in at least two places, and a twice-mended paw, she was too well-loved to be passed to another kid anyway.

Lily kissed the bear's sweet little embroidered nose—same as Bluebeary's, but darker brown—and remembered the Christmas she and Anders got them. In the days leading up to it, Lily had poked, hefted, jiggled, and squeezed every present waiting under the tree (a tree they'd cut down themselves from the woods behind the field, carrying it home on their shoulders, as they did every December), but she was most curious about two identical light, squishy gifts she guessed might have something Mom-made inside. She returned to those again and again, and desperately wanted to peek under the wrapping, but Anders forbade her from lifting even one tiny piece of tape. It was more fun to have the surprise, he said. It was most fun not knowing together. Since it was important to him, she tried to be patient.

On Christmas Eve eve, Lily couldn't take it any longer.

With Anders and Mom distracted by cookie dough, she snuck into the living room and slowly, gently lifted one corner of the shiny paper—just enough to see Bluebeary's fluffy left ear. Her pulse skipped. She loved him instantly.

She quickly reapplied the tape and hurried back into the kitchen, where Mom handed her a rolling pin and Anders shot her a curious glance. She smiled like nothing had happened, but she was buzzing with the secret she carried. Anders lifted his eyebrows and her excitement crash-landed. Guilt flooded in to replace it.

She'd betrayed him. Mom too. They both wanted the bears to be a surprise, and Lily had ruined it. She felt awful. She never peeked inside a present early again.

Lily squeezed Maude in a tight hug and wished that was the only time she'd failed her brother. She sucked in a ragged breath and buried her face in Maude's blue fur, surprised to find it wet against her cheeks. She pulled back and realized the dampness was tears—and the realization made her cry harder. What kind of sister was she, crying over a memory about teddy bears when she hadn't even cried over Anders' death?

She heard Mom's soft knock on the doorframe and collapsed against her, sobbing. Mom hugged her the way she'd been hugging Maude, and the tears and confession flew out of her.

"I should have told you," she said, tucked deep in Mom's

embrace, even though she didn't deserve it, even though Mom should hate her and probably would once all the words were out. "He passed out and I didn't tell you and he was sick and I didn't know but I did know and I could have saved him but I didn't and I covered it up and it's all my fault." She thought Mom might yell or push her away, but Mom didn't react, just kept holding her.

Maybe she'd said it too jumbled and Mom hadn't understood. She forced her shoulders to stop shaking and tried again. "It's my fault he died. I kept the secret. If I'd spoken up sooner, the doctors could have cured him. But I waited and the cancer spread. I hid it from you. I'm sorry."

Mom drew her closer and a few of her tears fell on Lily's scalp. "No," she said firmly. "It is not your fault. I promise. I know exactly how you feel because I blame myself too. But there is nothing you could have done to change this."

"But I—"

Mom shook her head. "You couldn't have stopped it. Nobody could. A terrible, horrible thing happened, but it did not happen because of you."

Lily drew a shaky breath and released it. Then another. And another. She leaned against Mom and believed her. "I miss him," she said, tears still streaming down her cheeks.

"Me too. We're always going to miss him," Mom said. Lily nodded. "We were so lucky to have him, and he was so lucky to have you. You know you were his favorite sister."

Lily smiled and said Anders' punch line: "And his worst."

Mom smiled too. "And his worst."

Lily sniffled and wiped her face on her sleeve. She shifted position but didn't pull out of the hug. It was nice, letting Mom take care of her. It was nice feeling comforted and loved.

"I'm sorry," Mom said. She ran her palm up and down Lily's back. Lily wanted her to never stop. "I'm sorry I didn't realize you carried that guilt. I'm sorry I haven't been the mother you've needed through all this. I love you, Lily. I'm so proud of who you are."

Lily snaked her arms around Mom's middle and squeezed. It was a good long time before she let go.

37

Tides of Change

"Listen, Safety Patrol," Quinn said. She tugged a pea-pod from the tall, tangled vines that grew between them, and dropped it into her basket. It was the third morning in a row that the chore of the day was gardening. In mid-August, everything was ripe.

"What?" Lily asked around a sweet, crunchy mouthful. Sugar snap peas were harder to spot than tomatoes or string beans because they were the exact same green as their vines and leaves, and liked to hide in them. They were also extremely delicious. Aunt Linda had said they could eat one pod for every ten they picked, but whenever Quinn talked, Lily lost count, so she hoped that had just been an estimate.

Maybe next year, she and Mom could plant a garden.

She bet Ms. Turner and Aunt Linda would be glad to help.

"Today and tomorrow are my last days of earning points for a while," Quinn said. "Soccer starts this weekend and I'll have practice every morning until school starts. Plus Sara's getting back from camp and Avery's job is done, so we'll be spending more time at Maddie's place. We go there to carbo-load. She loves to bake."

Lily swallowed and the news hit her stomach like a brick. "So . . . what does that mean for us? Will I ever see you again?" she asked.

Quinn smiled. "Lily, we live on an island. You'll see me everywhere, all the time, most likely."

Lily nodded, but she didn't fully believe it.

"Have you ever been to a soccer game?" Quinn asked. "You should come to our first home game. It's the Saturday after school starts. Bring your mom. We can use all the fans we can get. I always do best when people are rooting for me."

The brick of fear in Lily's gut dissolved. Cheering for Quinn at her soccer game did sound fun.

She resumed picking. "Maybe when you get your license you can drive me to school. Since I earned you all those points and stuff."

Quinn snorted. "Are you skipping three grades and starting high school?"

"No," Lily said.

"Then nope, not a chance. Though I do appreciate you."

Lily sighed. She'd figured it was a long shot. She ate another snap pea to compensate.

"Are you excited for school to start? And for seeing friends?" Quinn asked. She shifted down the row to the next pea plant. Lily followed.

"Not exactly," she admitted. "It will be weird to go back without Anders. Last spring was pretty bad. And I'm kind of dreading having to see my ex–best friend."

"Uh-oh," Quinn said. "What's the story there? You don't have to tell me if you don't want to," she added quickly.

"I don't mind." Lily recited what happened with Deandra at the party, and described how it felt, then and after.

Quinn listened quietly. She waited a beat after Lily was finished, and frowned a little, thinking. "Do you miss her?" she asked.

"No," Lily said. "I don't think so. I sort of miss the friend she was when we were little. When it was fun. But I don't think we've been like that for a while. I didn't really notice until this happened, but it's not the first time she's made me feel bad. I just . . . this time I couldn't shrug it off."

Quinn nodded, and the big, floppy hat Aunt Linda made her wear in the sun nodded with her. "You don't have to. If a friendship isn't working for you, you're allowed to step back. You can try to fix it if you want, but it's also perfectly okay to take a break," she said.

Lily looked at the ground. "I don't know if she even wants to be friends."

"Well, there you go," Quinn said. "Or maybe she does, but right now you can't force it."

Lily thought about that. It sounded true, and Quinn sounded certain, but she wasn't entirely sure what it meant. Or what she wanted it to mean for her and Deandra.

"Look," Quinn said. "Friends drift apart. And sometimes they drift back together. Other times they don't." Lily didn't know much about that, but she nodded so Quinn would keep talking.

"Like, take Payton and me." Quinn pointed a peapod at Lily for emphasis. "We hung out all the time in middle school. It was super intense, like joined at the hip. But this year we were more just part of the same group, not really one-on-one friends. And that's okay. Things shift. It might be forever, or it might not. My mom's still tight with her best friend from elementary school, but she says they barely even spoke when they were my age. Sometimes friendships have seasons, or come in and out like the tides."

Lily pictured her friendship with Deandra as a small oak tree growing in a clearing. Was it just dropping its leaves for winter, or did the whole tree need to be chopped down? She imagined a much sturdier pine tree, an evergreen, nearby. That pine could be her love for Anders. It stayed green even in winter and would always continue to grow.

"That's deep," she said. Quinn reached over the vines and swatted her shoulder. She giggled, but she hadn't meant to be sarcastic. Quinn had given her a lot to consider.

They picked in silence for a few minutes, and Lily earned four more peas by picking forty. Aunt Linda could feed the whole road with her garden.

"Tell me something random about Anders," Quinn said.

She looked up. "Like what?"

Quinn shrugged. "Up to you."

"Okay." She adjusted the brim of her Red Sox cap and said the first thing that came to mind. "He's freakishly good at ripping leaves into new shapes. Like, he can turn a maple leaf into a daisy or a shark or an octagon. When I try even a circle, the leaf just falls apart."

"That's a cool talent," Quinn said, and sounded like she meant it. So Lily told her something else.

"He makes fun of me whenever I use what he calls Lily Logic. That's when something makes perfect, obvious sense to me, but it's maybe not so obvious to everyone else."

Quinn grinned. "I've seen some Lily Logic in action," she said. "I love your weird brain."

Lily beamed. She told Quinn about wishing season and Us Things, and about how Anders always wrote in his spiral notebooks from front to back, like a normal person, but Lily wrote in hers from the back page to the front, because she was left-handed and didn't want the spiral getting in the way of her arm, so one time Lily thought Anders was pranking her by constantly moving her list book around the house, but really it was just that her list book was also his sketchbook, and neither of them noticed they were both using it because they'd been filling it from opposite ends.

Once she started talking about Anders, she couldn't stop. She wanted Quinn to know all about him. She wanted her friend to hold these memories of him too. The more stories she shared, the fuller she felt.

They were nowhere near the overlap, but it almost seemed like he was with them.

38

A New Plan

Lily tugged a wild blueberry off one of the reddish-green plants growing low to the ground toward the back of the field and popped it in her mouth. The tart-sweet juice exploded onto her tongue, more delicious than anything from a store. The berries were tiny but sun-warmed and packed with flavor. They were one of her favorite things about August.

She found another cluster, closer to dusky purple than blue. Picking berries in the field was like searching for jewels—an edible treasure hunt. In that moment, she was a dragon with black claws and shimmering wings, descending on a precious trove. She tipped back her head to breathe fire at the sky, then dropped a few berries into her shirt pocket for Mom, and a couple for Frankie, who loved them. It was too bad she couldn't share them with Anders.

He'd only come around for a few minutes today and seemed only half there at best. Lily wasn't surprised when she blinked and he was gone, but that didn't make it less disappointing.

Last night she'd found a book on one of Mom's shelves all about how babies develop. It described the growth of a normal fetus, week by week, and compared it to various fruits and household objects. Picturing a baby growing inside someone was weird enough—imagining it as a shoe or mango seemed unnecessary. But more disturbing was learning how slowly babies grow at first. A two-month-old fetus was only the size of a cherry and still scarcely recognizable as a future human. That scared her.

If Anders faded away at a similar rate to how he'd grown, she would barely see him in the two and a half months they figured he had left. Two and a half months was only ten or eleven weeks. An eleven-week-old fetus was no bigger than a Ping-Pong ball. By four weeks, it was as small as a speck of glitter.

Anders loved glitter. A sparkly exit would be perfect, except for how it involved him leaving her forever.

They no longer talked about that.

Their conversations were different these days. He listened, same as ever, but often didn't respond—at least, not out loud. Sometimes she felt his presence more than saw it, and had to just trust that he was there. She filled in the blanks with the words he wasn't saying. She told him things she wanted him to know, even if he might not remember.

It was a lot like the conversations Anders used to have with his favorite tree.

Nonetheless, he was the person she most wanted to talk to, especially now that Quinn was busy with soccer and no longer inviting Lily to do chores.

She knew what he would say about that: the same thing he'd been saying all along. She needed another friend.

Lily sighed and conceded the point. It was useless to keep arguing it in her head.

It was the topic they'd discussed most this past week in the overlap, with Lily voicing both their perspectives. They had reached an agreement of sorts. A new game plan.

Once school started, she would try speaking to people again, maybe. Or at least make eye contact. That would be a start.

If she saw Kenny, she would wave, like she'd promised. Lots of friendships began with hello.

But after talking it through with the person she loved most, and telling him everything she'd learned from Quinn, she had made a decision about Deandra: She couldn't go back to being friends, real friends, with someone who acted so careless of her feelings. It was more than just one moment—it was a pattern Lily didn't want to be part of. She was done being close to someone who hurt her and never even tried to apologize.

But not being friends didn't mean they had to be enemies. It was exhausting to hold that grudge. And with only twenty-two other kids in their entire grade, Lily couldn't exactly avoid her forever.

What Deandra had said was messed up, but messing up wasn't unforgivable.

As long as Deandra didn't act mean, Lily would take a page from Anders' book and let the bad stuff go. They could be friendly without being friends. A dragon could afford to be slightly generous.

Lily swished her spiky tail. Her rainbow scales glinted in the sun. She was fierce. She was brave. And she could do this.

39

A Mysterious Missive

The mailbox was empty when Lily returned from her morning visit with Ms. Turner and the chickens, but that was only because Mom had already taken the mail inside. In the spot in the kitchen where Lily normally placed bills and letters for Mom, a single envelope waited. Lily's name was on the front.

She frowned and picked it up. She was not in the mood for more credit card offers, but this seemed like it might contain something else. The long white envelope was shaped the same as those others, but this time her name and address were handwritten, not typed, and whoever wrote them— someone in Texas, according to the postmark over the red flower stamp—had done so in purple pen.

But who did she know in Texas? She ripped open the back to find out.

The letter she unfolded was also written in purple, with slanted cursive on lined paper. She glanced at the signature at the bottom of the page and did not recognize the name. She read the whole thing from the top.

Dear Lily,

I removed your name and address from the credit card company's mailing list, and I'm sorry you received that offer in the first place. You're right that it never should have been sent. I work in the office that opens the mail, not the one that sends it, but I apologize on behalf of all of us for the mix-up with your name. I can imagine how much it hurt to see that.

I don't know all the ways you have felt since your brother died, but I might know some of it, because I lost my older sister when we were teenagers, and I've missed her every day since.

It has been over two decades since Leslie died, but I still see her eyes light up when her favorite song comes on the radio. I still hear her voice in my head, offering opinions about outfits, politics, movie stars, and everything else. (She always had a lot of opinions.) When I see the word "spaghetti," I remember the terrible fake Italian accent she would use to make me laugh, and it still makes me laugh. She's still my goofy, opinionated, headstrong big sister, even though she's gone. I've never met anyone like her.

When Leslie died, it was hard to believe I would be able to keep going. My grief was so enormous, it seemed to fill me up. There was no space in me for anything besides it.

Time passed, and my grief didn't shrink. It's still just as big. But day by day, month by month, year by year, I've grown and expanded around it. I have space in me now for all the ways I feel about Leslie, but I have space for other things too. In times when it's felt like I might burst, I grew a little more. I'm still growing.

I know your heart is growing every day too, Lily. You're going to fill it up with a lifetime of amazing, wonderful things. Anders is one of those things—a very important one. You will always carry him with you. May his memory be a blessing.

Sincerely yours,
Miriam

A tear dropped from Lily's eye and splatted on the page. She wiped the dampness from her cheeks and read the note again, then again. Each time she read the letter, her heart expanded a little more.

Miriam was right. There was space inside her for many things, and Anders would always be one of them. But there would be chickens and Qwirkle and sixth grade and snap peas, and who knew whatever else to come, too.

She folded the letter, took it upstairs, and tucked it into her notebook for safekeeping.

40

Moving in Squiggles

On the first afternoon of summer, Lily didn't think ahead as far as August. If she had, she would have assumed that in the last couple weeks before school began, she would spend as many hours, minutes, and seconds as she could in the overlap with Anders. She hadn't known he would hardly be there.

She was grateful for that—for the months of just being together, having fun, before she worried about losing him again.

Normally, by late August, she would be eager for the school year to start—looking forward to fresh notebooks, unused erasers, fat textbooks, and shiny-clean whiteboards. It was tough to get excited about school supplies while bracing for a year without Anders in it. But she didn't entirely regret that sixth grade was coming.

"Honestly, it will probably be a good distraction," she said aloud, kicking the ground with her heels to make the tire swing move faster. In the branches above her, the crab apples were beginning to ripen. In another month, she and Mom could collect them to make cider. "No offense, but talking to ghosts can't be my only hobby."

She didn't glance toward the spot where she'd glimpsed Anders in her peripheral vision—he seemed to stick around longer if she didn't look directly at him—but she felt he was there, and that he agreed with her declarations. She'd never had to look at him to sense what he was thinking or feeling, and that was especially useful now that he was so difficult to see.

"Maybe I'll take up embroidery," she said, and felt Anders smile. The winter he got into needlepoint, she'd given up on her third try at just threading the needle. She wasn't patient enough for sewing—or for most things she wasn't instantly good at. She preferred messier craft projects anyway, like papier-mâché or collage.

"Or I'll try stamp collecting. Or underwater basket weaving," she added. "Actually, underwater basket weaving would probably be fun."

She wished he could tease her out loud.

Now that she couldn't spend mornings with Quinn, she

took her time eating breakfast and visiting the chickens. Sometimes she brought a book up the hill and sat to read in the shade of the shed. Today she drank iced tea with Ms. Turner in her kitchen and they traded interesting facts, like that an ostrich's eye is bigger than its brain, and it's illegal to sing in public while wearing a swimsuit in Florida.

But in the afternoons, she had more time for missing him. If Mom went to the store for groceries or to the post office to mail projects she'd sold, Lily volunteered to go with her. A couple times she saw someone she recognized from school and, remembering the game plan, said hey. They always said hey back.

Quinn's prediction that they would see each other everywhere seemed true. They'd already run into each other once at Burnt Cove Market with their moms, and Lily spotted Quinn another time with her friends downtown, hanging out on the library steps with iced coffees from 44 North. Lily gave a subtle wave in case Quinn didn't want to be outed as friends with a sixth grader, but Quinn immediately called her over and introduced her to Nolan and Mads. They didn't act like it was weird that Quinn knew her. In fact, they were nice. It made Lily feel three inches taller.

The end of August was, as usual, quite busy in town, with lots of tourists and summer people around. It was the time of year when locals looked forward to the drop in temperature and change of seasons that would send most visitors home—except for leaf peepers, who drove slowly down the narrow roads in September and October to witness the turning foliage. Anders used to make her and Mom laugh by gripping an imaginary steering wheel and pretending to peer out a car window, shouting, "Look, Myrtle! That one's turning red!" She smiled at the memory, though she hated that he wouldn't be doing that this year.

Five days before the start of sixth grade, Lily stepped outside, turned right back around, and went upstairs for a sweatshirt. Unless the chickens wanted to share their down feathers with her, she would need it. September mornings were chilly.

As she pulled the sweatshirt over her head, she heard a muffled, familiar sound and her heart twinged. She had thought Mom was doing better.

There were so many good signs, like how the pile of mail in the kitchen had shrunk, and the carpet had vacuum lines for the first time in ages. Like how they ate their own food now instead of things the neighbors brought over. Like how Mom's smile reached her eyes, which weren't always red from crying. But she was crying now in Anders' room, as sad as ever.

Lily straightened her sweatshirt and tiptoed out of her

bedroom. Mom probably wanted privacy, and Lily didn't want to get stuck in her sorrow.

Halfway down the stairs, she paused. She thought of Ms. Weed, the school guidance counselor, who pulled her out of class a few times "just to talk," which meant Ms. Weed talking while Lily sat there, mostly silent, occasionally shrugging if Ms. Weed asked a question. Ms. Weed had said grief doesn't move in a straight line, but in squiggles, sometimes looping back around to where it started. She'd said, over and over, it was okay to not be okay.

The words hadn't meant much to Lily at the time, but she understood them differently now.

If Ms. Weed invited Lily to her office to talk again this fall, maybe Lily would tell her about the squiggles. Maybe it was okay if Mom was squiggling right now. Maybe Lily could hug her through it.

She walked back up the steps and curled up on Anders' bed. Mom cuddled against her and sniffled, and they both felt sad, but for once, Lily didn't try to avoid it. It was nice, in a way, to just feel it. And there was comfort in feeling it together. Mom's breathing steadied as her tears slowed, and Lily felt useful and glad.

"You know what I miss?" Lily said after a few minutes. "I miss random tackles and wrestling together."

Mom laughed with a small hiccup. "You two were like

puppies. No—little tiger cubs. I knew siblings bickered, but I never expected you to roughhouse and tumble so much."

Lily grinned, picturing Anders with stripes and a tail. Maybe she would be a tiger cub for Halloween. "Did you ever wish you had a sibling?" she asked.

"I wanted one sometimes. An older sister, especially. But I also liked having Mimi to myself."

"Plus you had Barkly," she pointed out.

"That's true, I did."

"Maybe we should get a dog," Lily said, and waited for Mom to reply like she always did: that a dog would be too much of a nuisance.

But Mom said "Hmm" and nodded slowly. "Maybe we should."

Lily pounced. "I would take really, really good care of one. I'd be even better with a dog than I am with the chickens. I'll do all her walks and feeding and brushing and everything. And teach her tricks. She'll be so well trained. Not a nuisance at all."

Mom smiled and ruffled her hair. "Let me think about it, okay?"

"Really?"

"Really, I'll think about it. That wasn't a yes. But a dog might be nice for both of us," Mom said.

Lily tried not to squeal. A maybe was practically a yes.

After all those years of begging—Anders wasn't going to believe it. But she knew now was not the time to push.

She settled back into the cuddle and felt the steady rise and fall of Mom's chest. She adjusted her own breaths so they inhaled and exhaled together.

"I talk to him sometimes," she said, breaking the quiet. "Out by the tire swing. It feels like he's there with me."

The confession spun out of Lily's reach. Her secret glimmered, unprotected in the light.

Maybe she shouldn't have told Mom the truth.

She held very still, like a rabbit afraid of a predator, but Mom didn't laugh or dismiss what she'd said. She gave Lily a light squeeze. "I'm glad," she said, and kissed her temple.

Lily relaxed. She gazed at an open box on the floor with Anders' T-shirts folded inside. One of his favorites was on top. It said *Visualize Whirled Peas*. She wished she could wrap herself and Mom in its soft, well-worn fabric, and include Anders in the cuddle too.

She sat up. "Hey, Mom?"

"Yes?"

"What if instead of giving away his clothes, we made them into something else?"

Mom blinked. "Like what?"

"Like maybe a blanket we can wrap ourselves in. A quilt that's also a hug. One with good memories stitched in."

She could picture it already and the idea made her bounce. This was a project she wouldn't mind threading needles for. She'd sew patiently all winter if that was what it took.

Mom's eyes filled with tears, but her smile stayed. "I think that will be wonderful."

41

Scraps and Pieces

They got started right away. The first task was to sort through Anders' clothes and choose which ones to include. Lily had the idea to mix pieces cut from his shirts, pants, and pajamas with some of his favorite fabrics in Mom's collection, so they went through her scrap bin too.

Once the fabrics were assembled, they selected threads in contrasting colors. Next came sketching ideas and designs for how they might piece everything together. There was a lot to decide and prep before even a single stitch got made.

Lily and Mom worked on the quilt in the mornings after breakfast—sometimes with music on; sometimes in quiet or just talking. In the afternoons, Lily went to the overlap and described every detail of how it was going. If she had time after that, she visited the chickens. After dinner, she and Mom worked a bit more.

Lily dreamed of flannel stars, corduroy hearts, and flowers cut from cotton. She studied stitches and appliqués, played with shapes, and invented patterns. She got so wrapped up in the project, she almost forgot to be nervous about sixth grade approaching. But as the bus chugged up the hill to get her to the first day, she remembered.

She remembered, and her shoes got heavy, and her skin began to sweat.

The bus heaved to a stop and its doors squeaked open. Clara, the same bus driver Lily had for fifth grade, peered down at her and grunted. "You coming up?" Clara asked. Clara wasn't known for being warm and fuzzy.

Lily wiped her palms on her jeans and took a very deep breath before climbing the steps to board. Clara shut the doors behind her and put the bus in gear.

Lily's chest fluttered with nerves as she started down the aisle. As a sixth grader, she had rights to the seats pretty far back, but the path to get there seemed eternal, and she could feel Clara's impatience building. Lily wasn't quite ready to be back there with the other middle schoolers, anyway. She saw an open seat three rows behind the driver and took it.

The bus rolled forward. Lily exhaled. She was on her way.

She watched out the window as the bus passed the pond,

climbed the hill, and flew by Ms. Turner's road. It rounded a curve and slowed, then stopped to let on another passenger.

A tiny kid in a button-up shirt scaled the steps like they were huge boulders. He glanced around, as wide-eyed as a bullfrog, before darting into the empty seat across from Lily's. She saw his moms and younger brother wave good-bye from where they'd been waiting with him at the end of their dirt road, but the tiny kid didn't wave back. He stared straight ahead and clutched his hands in his lap, as frozen as that deer she'd seen in the moonlight.

Lily leaned toward the aisle. "Hey," she said.

The kid jolted and shot her a nervous look. She remembered how enormous and scary sixth graders had once seemed to her and Anders. She smiled to reassure him she was friendly.

"First day of kindergarten?" she guessed. The bus stopped and let two more students on. They moved toward the back of the bus, shouting and laughing.

The tiny kid nodded slightly.

"Cool," Lily said. "Kindergarten's great. You'll learn lots of new things and make lots of new friends."

The kid fidgeted. Lily wasn't sure if she was helping.

"I'm starting sixth grade," she said. "And I've heard it's great too. But if you want to know the truth, I'm a little nervous," she admitted.

The kid eyed her suspiciously. "But you're old!" he protested.

"True," Lily said. "But new beginnings can be scary for
anyone."

The kid nodded, and Lily felt very wise. She was glad he
seemed to be loosening.

"What are you most excited for today?" she asked.

He bit his lip, thinking. "Recess," he said. "And writing
books."

Lily hid her grin. If the kid thought he'd be writing
whole books on the first day of kindergarten, he was in for a
real disappointment. It was good to dream big though.

"I like books too," she said. "I'm looking forward to
finding out what we'll be reading this year. And seeing how
everyone changed over the summer." The bus turned right
and made its way past the high school, up the elementary
school's long driveway, which seemed too short today, to
Lily. "Hey, what's your name?" she asked the kid, to distract
herself.

"Elliot," he replied.

"Elliot, I'm Lily," she said as the bus approached the
drop-off spot. "Thanks for keeping me company on the bus
ride. You've earned ten points."

Elliot brightened. "Really?" he said, as enthusiastic as
Achoo got when Lily brought scraps to the hens.

"Really," Lily said.

"Cool!" Elliot jumped up, looking pleased and proud. He raced off the bus without even asking what the points went toward.

Lily stood, put on her backpack, and awarded herself ten points too. She smiled shyly at two classmates who were coming up the aisle, said "thank you" to Clara as she made her way off the bus, and walked into the new school year, a little surer and more eager with each step.

42

Wishing in the Wind

When the bus brought her home nearly eight hours later, Lily dropped her backpack in the dooryard and flew.

The afternoon sun slanted low across the field. Each blade it touched shone like Rumpelstiltskin had spun it to gold. Lily sat on the swing in the overlap and looked up.

Long white trails of a long-gone airplane thinned from stripes to wisps as the vapor spread across the sky. She imagined how tiny her home must look from so many miles above it. She had never been on an airplane. But none of those travelers had been on her tire swing, or even to the island, most likely. The planes on that flight path were headed to Europe, all the way across the whole ocean.

The wind brushed her cheeks and rustled the trees' first bursts of red, yellow, and orange. She would take a trip like that someday, she decided. A grand adventure. She would leave and return to tell Anders and Mom all about it.

Even once Anders was gone, he would always be here. He was part of this place, as much as the sounds and the scents and the breeze. She couldn't see those things either, but she felt them.

"Sixth grade is okay," she said to him now. "I didn't, like, make a new best friend or discover uranium or whatever, but it wasn't bad. It was mostly tolerable." She sensed a movement to her left and subtly glanced in that direction, but it was only a white-throated sparrow. She looked away.

"I'm not a ghost anymore. I mean, nobody treated me like one." She paused. "Maybe now that you're more ghostly I'm more solid or something." She felt him appreciate that.

She twisted back and forth in the tire swing and considered what he would want to know. "I sat with Kenny and Ashlynn at lunch," she reported. "We had fish sticks. Ashlynn's wicked funny. Did you know she plays ukulele? I told her I play fart hand and she said we should do a duet." She giggled. "Maybe for the holiday talent show. Her oldest sister is on the soccer team with Quinn, so she'll be at the game this weekend too."

Her smile faltered. "Deandra's best friends with Taylor

now, I guess. Which is fine. I still need someone to sit with on the bus though."

The breeze picked up and her stomach grumbled. She sat a little longer, then stood. She needed a snack, and the crab apples were still too sour to eat. "I miss you," she said. "And you're missing first-day spaghetti tonight. Mom remembered. She even put it on the shopping list herself." The sparrow chirped at her from a low branch of the apple tree. She ignored it. "We're cutting the triangle pieces for the quilt after dinner. Or probably some of them. There are a lot of those."

The golden grasses of the field rippled in the wind, moving like the surface of the ocean. Lily watched them and had a sudden thought. "Wait. In Rumpelstiltskin, what's the miller's daughter's name? Does Rumpelstiltskin ever try to find out?" She narrowed her eyes, thinking. "She's called 'the miller's daughter,' then she's 'the queen,' but does anyone guess *her* name? I don't think it's in the book."

Anders didn't answer, but she assumed he didn't know. "I'll report back when I find out," she said, and turned away. "Later, alligator."

Three steps later, she froze. There, at what used to be the edge of the overlap, was a perfectly puffy white dandelion, just waiting, like a gift. She picked it with a small smile. Wishing season was still going.

The dandelion's seeds flew off as she blew. Some twirled to the ground; others danced with the wind. As they floated and dispersed, Lily thought about hope—about cycles and seasons and new flowers growing. How endings are also beginnings.

She didn't have words for what she wished, but she knew that Anders could feel it.

43

Where Wishes Land

At the edge of the woods, where the grasses grew long, near the path to the stream and soft moss beds, a red fox with a bushy tail lifted her nose in the air and sniffed. Her ears twitched.

The wind smelled of the girl who often played in this spot and who must have been there just moments ago. Her scent was receded and fading, though the hope in it lingered.

There was something else there too, the fox noticed. More extraordinary. Harder to pinpoint.

It was the presence of the boy who belonged with the girl—not the scent of him, but the sense. He was there but also not. The fox's vision was sharp and even her keen eyes couldn't spot him. But she knew for certain he'd been with her.

No matter. The girl and the boy were no threat to the fox, nor the kits who would soon leave her den. They were still only kits themselves.

A dandelion seed tickled the fox's whiskers and landed on the tip of her snout. She sneezed and returned to the forest. The girl's wish continued on its way.

44

The Shape of a Heart

At almost exactly the usual time, the school bus rolled to its usual stop, wheezed open its doors, and coughed out a girl. She jumped to the gravel with a giggle.

The girl looked up and waved to a friend in the window before crossing in front of the flashing red lights and hurrying up the slope toward home. As the ground flattened out, her shoes crunched fallen leaves that covered the autumn-brown grass. She ran to the door of the big white house, smiling as she approached it. The gap-toothed jack-o'-lanterns on the step smiled back.

The girl opened the door and a dog bounded out, wagging his fluffy white tail. "Sit, Nuisance!" she said, and the dog sat. "Good dog." She kneeled and the dog licked her chin.

The girl scratched behind the dog's soft, floppy ears, and stroked his black-and-white fur. He wriggled with delight and rolled over in the leaves to offer his belly for petting. She obliged.

With the belly rub complete, the girl and dog stood and shook off the leaves that stuck to them. The dog turned toward the door, his eyes shining brightly, but the girl didn't follow. She bent to retrieve something off the ground she had noticed as it was falling.

It was a dark red maple leaf, torn into the shape of a heart, and blown there by the wind.

The girl held the leaf by its stem and admired it for a long moment before slipping it into her pocket. "I miss you too," she whispered. She wiped her cheeks on her sleeve.

The girl and the dog went inside the warm house, and the door closed gently behind them.

Acknowledgments

Enormous thanks to my editor, Rosemary Brosnan, and my agent, Michael Bourret, without whom this book would be half as long, twice as sad, and sorely lacking in chickens. I'm so lucky to have each of you by my side, helping my wishes come true.

Thanks to Caitlin Lonning for her discerning eye(s) and thoughtful queries, and to Courtney Stevenson for continuously being the best. I'm grateful to everyone at Quill Tree Books and HarperCollins who devotes their time and talent to my books, including the wonderful marketing, sales, publicity, design, and sub rights teams.

Thanks to Robin Wasserman for listening to my woes, encouraging my delusions, and breaking things open with the suggestion of rabbits. Thank you, Amy Jo Burns, for bringing your brilliant, beautiful heart to every loop of this park we've been walking together. Hugs to the always-inspiring Mice & Uteruses: A-M McLemore, Emily X.R. Pan, and Nova Ren Suma, who make Thursdays immeasurably better. Extra bubbles and ice cream to all the friends I've leaned on during this process, including Alex Arnold, Bree Barton, Terry J. Benton-Walker, Alison Cherry, Jill Day, Sarah Dodge, Erin Soderberg Downing, Nora Ericson, Lainie Fefferman, Andrew Garrison, Sarah Gersick, Corey Ann Haydu, Sulaiman Ijaz, Maxine Kaplan, Helen Kim, Claire Legrand, Kendra Levin, Tiff Liao, Margaret Meyers, Jascha Narveson, Sophie Danis Oberfield, Max Perelman, Abby Ranger, Sarah Nicole Smetana, Gavin Steingo, Lauren Strasnick, and the ever-sparkling Terra Elan McVoy. Love to Rachel Pilling, Rebekah Sirois, and Sanders Weirs-Haggerty—for every other Tuesday and the times before, between, and forthcoming.

Thanks to Island Readers & Writers, Princeton Public Library, Stonington Public Library, Labyrinth Books, Maine Writers & Publishers Alliance, and all the hardworking educators, booksellers, and librarians who connect books with readers and readers with books.

Thank you to my parents for the barn, field, pond, granite, ocean, moss, pines, mushrooms, lupines, frogs, crab apples, sunsets, goose poop, music, and tire swing, and for the gift of time and space to write. Hugs to Erika, Anna, Sophia, and Harper. Thanks to Uncle Markus for the purple chair and sturdy desk. Thank you, Jeff, for listening to it all out loud and helping me stay flatted. Belly rubs to Tato. One last kiss on the snout for my Rooga. And a huge Deer Isle smile just for you, Jeremy.

Thank you, Deer Isle: the community and landscape that shaped me, and the neighbors and friends within it (including the kid on Dunham Point Road who kindly answered my questions about his chickens). Every time I cross the bridge, my heart shifts back into place. The island will always be home.